Alex and the Color of the Wind

To Nell.
[illegible]
[illegible]
for Sailing Boats
[illegible] June 2008

ALSO BY PIERO RIVOLTA

Sunset in Sarasota
Just One Scent, the Rest is God

Alex
and the Color
of the Wind

Piero Rivolta

NEW CHAPTER
PUBLISHER

Published by New Chapter Publisher

ISBN 978-0-9792012-1-9

New Chapter Publisher
1765 Ringling Blvd.
Suite 300
Sarasota, FL 34236
941-954-0355

Originally published as *Alex e il Colore del Vento* by Bietti, Milan, Italy, November 2003

Alex and the Color of the Wind is available for sale at:
   www.newchapterpublisher.com
   www.amazon.com

Printed in the United States of America

Cover Design by Shaw Creative

To Rachele.
The boat or the woman?

It was the hour that turns seafarers' longings homeward the hour when their hearts grow tender upon the day they bid sweet friends farewell

– Dante, *The Divine Comedy*

Part One

Chapter 1

It's foggy, but now and again sharp bands of golden light appear. A patch of sky breaks through, then more fog, sky, rays of light.

How strange!

It's like seeking, finding, thinking, building enthusiasm and thinking it over again.

Walking along the beach in such a mood induces you to reflect upon the experience of a lifetime, all concentrated in the few hours of one morning.

This is what he thought after leaning his bike up against the trunk of a palm tree behind the low dune, heading south on foot, wherever the beach might take him. Every so often he would pick up a shell or a piece of one, examine it and toss it away after considering how destiny drags things and men around this world at will.

But what is the will of destiny? Difficult question.

Perhaps he could have asked the sky, but just then more fog rolled in, and the sky could not be seen. The fog, of course, would make no answer – it only steals away thoughts and hides them who knows where.

Yet he knew those thoughts were real; he felt them living inside of him.

He had the sensation that they were doggedly trying to get out.

But it was foggy outside, and this lack of a clear-cut dimension may have discouraged them – coming out could mean being stolen away and hidden. Hidden where?

In reality, he thought, it's not the fog that hides thoughts, but humanity – in its desire that it be buried in the sand, where it is safe and strikes no fear in the world. The sand, though, is rife with creatures that dig holes of every shape and size. And no matter how microscopic those openings may be, thoughts manage to escape in tiny haggard groups. Wet and chilled as they are, they feel weak and somewhat confused. Thus it will take them quite a while to reorganize and find the strength to set off and circulate throughout the world.

Their tribulations are not over, however, because the world, seeing what bad shape they are in, does not immediately take them into consideration. It takes years and even centuries for the world to note their presence, assess them, and ultimately recognize them as an integral part of itself.

"Look how many things you can figure out on the beach as the sun rises warm and slow and clears the fog."

He caught himself thinking out loud, in the hopes of remembering these inane reflections. By the time the sun had made its way through the fog, it would already have brought along the whole blue sky and expanse of turquoise sea to the white beaches made of the remains of seashells that reflect light like spring snow, compact and crusty, covering the soft hills at the foot of jagged mountains. The kind of snow that makes you feel light, almost weightless, when you ski on it, coasting along the surface, barely making a crack. Meanwhile you keep wondering suspiciously – when will it give in under my weight? At any rate, you keep gliding across crystals of snow that shine in the sun's rays and through the crackling of the minuscule breaks made by your skis in the thin layer of ice that protects the snow below.

You realize that these dry, barely perceptible sounds reach your ears amplified, and that your every sense perceives them with strange intensity.

It's as if you were a famous chef at an important gathering, with the eyes of all present upon you, as you decorate – with a phrase or a scene – a large cream-filled cake with a crispy caramel frosting. Careful! The coating must not be broken; there's no way or time to make another.

The skis glide, you listen and consider all with genuine satisfaction – what pleasure!

The intensity of your perception increases as you become ever more aware that your actions rest in a precarious balance. The further down the slope you go, the greater the chances of a sudden change in temperature or humidity that would weaken the consistency of the crust.

You can already see yourself with skis wallowing in the thick, heavy, snowy cream below the surface. But each minute you go on is more infused with the sweet taste of victory.

It's true: pleasures are beautiful and intense only when they carry within them the awareness of their own precariousness. Then they slip away, and you live in memories and the near certainty that you'll experience them again one day, at another time, in another place. Or perhaps you will experience these magical moments all at once – though you haven't the least idea where or when.

Now, as the sun manifests itself in all its tropical vigor, the beach is pearly white, the sky azure, the sea turquoise. And so they will remain the whole day through.

He returned to his bike and rode home.

At home he changed into some less comfortable clothes for work at the office.

When it came down to it, the office was his world.

He thought, "You have to convince yourself you like it, but it's not that hard."

Chapter 2

He turned the corner at the last intersection before the office. The car was spacious. Its air conditioner did a careful and precise job maintaining internal temperature and humidity at extremely pleasant levels – a constant though artificial spring.

Outside the sun blazed clear and bright.

Music at a fairly high volume filled the interior, so that each note reverberated. It became like a dialogue between the driver and Beethoven. Beethoven can be a friend or almost a psychologist who seems to know how to fit different situations like a glove. More often he listened to Brahms while driving – music that stimulated his sensory perception of the things that surrounded him. When, on the other hand, he felt the need to experience stormy seas, broken dreams or languidness, he put on a Verdi CD.

Basically, every morning he tried to listen to something that, in that moment, gave him the sensation of being able to co-exist with those sounds. Thus he passed from Verdi to Dvořák to Saint-Saëns, from Chopin to Liszt, from Paganini to Rossini, and so on.

But let's return to that corner at the intersection – there's the office. It's located in a respectable, well-proportioned building. The thing that counts most in a building is proportion. The taste in the details may change, time may take its toll and erode and sometime soften graceless and flawless particulars alike.

What remains that impacts the lives of city dwellers over the years are forms and the relationships that unite them: simplicity, fluidity, harmony of volume, the clarity of the message that the building must convey, its functionality, and the balance between costs and manifestations of wealth linked to the particular use it is intended for.

Strangely enough, all these elements and more, which are considered during a building's planning stages, seem to impregnate it to such a point as to create an actual language. Though its details are often not understood, this language influences the way passers-by perceive its impact.

The building where his office is located is quadrangular and rises four floors above the parking area, which occupies the ground floor. There is more parking around the building, immersed in tropical vegetation. The overall aspect conveys a sense of balance, and there are several reminders of northern Mediterranean traditions.

It is a style very different from those bizarre Hispanic-French-Italian combinations that were all the rage in Florida during the period at the turn of the millennium. Homes and apartment buildings with many – too many – roofs rife with pinnacles, and tall and spindly or thick and outlandish columns. Upon entering, you discover rooms with ceilings so high that you feel like you're having your usual cocktail or glass of wine in a gothic church.

As he parked, he thought of all these things. He was an architect who, along with his firm, specialized in industrial design as well as construction.

How many of these strange architectural jumbles had he designed to keep the customers happy, and to make his company grow and flourish!

It's much harder to create a "good" building, one that is inconspicuous precisely because it is "good."

It might be a success for the architect who designed it, but a disaster for the real estate agent who has to sell it! Surely it appears smaller, less pretentious, and since it blends with its surroundings, it can even go totally unnoticed. Clients who prefer this type of building are rarer all the time.

He felt a certain satisfaction as he entered his building. There was always a serene but active atmosphere inside.

Passing by the computer stations and various offices, he felt the human warmth and liveliness which seems to become almost palpable when a group of individuals dedicates its minds professionally and passionately to work. This situation is often encountered in small firms engaged in non-repetitive activities.

He felt gratified. To lighten the daily routine, it's important to be able to maintain such ideal conditions.

After all, one spends more time at the office or thinking up solutions to problems than, say, "having fun."

All it takes is adapting the concept of "having fun" to another type of use – apply it to work, and see existence transformed into a magical experience and receive pleasure from one's daily commitments.

He had pretty much arrived at such a conception by instinct, without asking too many questions or making precise plans.

Now, however, he was more aware of it, and more often than ever before he would catch himself pondering the various periods of his life.

He recalled his happy and vibrant youth, when he had lived at home with his parents. But in Europe, and even more so in Italy, where he was born, living had become difficult, burdened with rules and rivalries which spurred the creation of even more absurd rules.

It was all justified by self-styled "great movements of thought" based on highly debatable principles, heralded by mediocre and shortsighted men who were gifted with a misguided cunning of the sort that proposed, "Let's slaughter the cow that provides the community with milk. I don't have to worry, since I'm friends with my neighbor and he never lets me go without milk because he has his own cow."

Unfortunately, at that particular point in history, such ideas had numerous supporters.

People weren't, and perhaps still aren't, ready to perceive all of life's colors and draw from them inspiration for dealing simply and professionally with problems that crop up every hour, every day, every month, every year, every decade, and so on.

The tendency was much more simplistic: Follow a political or religious creed which in itself contained the theoretical solution to every ill. But that was just a mockery of reality that led to a perpetuation of mistakes. The evolution of a people is slow; perhaps it is and will always remain a mere illusion. Positive cycles seem to be followed by periods of progressive destruction of goals attained.

Having the chance to start over is a great pleasure, a challenge alluring to everyone. It is necessary to evolve, even in the awareness that one risks returning to where one started from. This too is a change, perhaps a rediscovery or even a recycling of ideas – but it is, in any case, evolution.

The nuances might be different; life's colors might become now more faint, now more intense. One's approach to the great mystery of death might be more gripping or detached. Love, hate, the sea, the earth, the sky, art, science, beliefs may be experienced to a greater or lesser degree; but the human spirit can still remain open to change and experience it with lucidity.

The worst damage a generation can do is to influence its heirs with so-called "surefire beliefs." In the end, it's only a weakness, an attempt to reassure or convince ourselves that such beliefs do actually work and are truly "safe."

Instead, the only sure things are problems that need solving every day, if possible with simplicity and intelligence.

Experience, beliefs, culture – an entire patrimony accumulated – these are positive elements, but you also have to be ready to evolve, or stand aside and watch, perhaps even shaking a finger. Why would anybody want to obstruct the course of evolution, which, compared to the duration of human existence, seems to go round and round, endlessly reinventing itself?

He lingered amid his reflections as he organized his work station to start the day. He sloughed off his contemplative haze to exchange a few kind, jocular words with his assistant. In an efficient organization there's always an assistant hard at work, with delicacy and precision. Of course, she makes mistakes, but she knows how to share them and find a solution to remedy both her own shortcomings and those of her boss. She is able to transform any snag into a strong point – an essential condition for playing "the game of work" in a constructive fashion.

Basically, he was happy, inasmuch as a human being could be.

He was 48 years old and had lived the past 29 in the United States. He'd nearly forgotten his real name. Everyone called him Alex – a blending and phonetic re-elaboration of the vowels and consonants of the first name on his birth certificate.

That morning the past had vanished like the fog.

Strange, fog was an extremely rare occurrence along Florida's west coast – it came perhaps only three or four times a year. It was always an intense experience for Alex, though.

That cottony mist reminded him of his youth. But then would come the sun's golden rays, like swords slicing through the fog, and reveal the white sand and the sea. The fusion of all these phenomena belonged to his second life. In the fog of his youth there was no white sand or sea, and the sun gave off a different heat, with an almost Nordic taste to it.

Changing continents, moving from Europe to America, making new friends, adapting to new customs, inventing a new livelihood for himself and building a new home – it is a little like living a second life. The bad thing is the sensation that your life is somehow shorter, or at any rate has gone by much more quickly. The first part is perceived as if it were another thing, a memory lived intensely. The second part is like hopping in a car that's already cruising down the road in third gear – there are two more, but both are fast, too fast to enjoy with the attention they deserve.

But by now, that was that. Time had flown, decisions had been made, which were now being carried out.

Deep down he felt proud of having made the leap into this new life with a certain amount of success, and proud that he fit in so well with the new system.

He was at a loss, though, to say how he had actually come to land on the west coast of Florida.

He took the usual route from Europe to New York. For many years he worked in that city – where all the languages of the world are spoken, where realities very different from one another exist side-by-side, realities still linked to their origins but at the same time Americanized. It's extraordinary how they co-exist, in a great upheaval, playing and clashing with one another, like fireworks across the sky.

A strange city! It's like walking into a store in outer space and saying, "I'd like a sample of human activity on earth. A sample that explains a bit of everything, a condensed edition, something like *Reader's Digest*. Later I'll make a more in-depth study."

If such a store existed, they'd have to furnish their customers with a detailed video of life in New York. By examining the city's inhabitants and their customs, one would get an idea of the complex madness that goes into the making of humankind. What's more, it's madness that's sought out, desired and defended with pride. On the basis of this sample, one might come up with a more detailed plan and dabble in the variations of co-existence in different locations throughout the world, back to the origins of the single ingredients that make up the great hodgepodge of our common existence.

Initially, Alex worked as an architect, but the profession was too limited for his character, overly subject to rules and regulations. Over time, his professional horizons had broadened; he began designing and developing all sorts of objects – including furniture, interiors of boats, and more. He began traveling throughout the United States for work, and expanded to Canada and Latin America. Lately he had even begun working with Asian firms and traveling to Southeast Asia. All this globe-trotting, however, had never wiped away his memory of old Europe, where his roots lay, where he still loved to make short but sweet return stops every now and then.

Europe, what a strange concept! It was only here, in America, that one spoke of Europe as an entity situated across the ocean, with whom there was a close bond of kinship. Americans from the United States influence Europe, but Europeans also influence America. We think, without ever admitting it and with a fair amount of rivalry, that by struggling together, both carry onward the tradition of "Western Culture." But in Europe, despite economic integration, the convergence of individual national legislations and the lack of customs duties, such awareness disappears.

You're a part of Europe, so you must be European, but then you realize there are German Europeans, French Europeans, Spanish Europeans, Italian Europeans, and so on. Much of the time they're forced to speak English just to understand one another, which brings us to the British Isles. Question: Are the inhabitants of these islands Europeans, or English, Irish, Scottish, Welsh? Whatever they are, they're also first cousins to the Americans, with whom they enjoy a typically stormy but close relationship.

Really, though, why worry? This is reality. Europe lies across the ocean, and for the next few decades at least, it's highly unlikely that the deeply rooted sentiments in Europeans are about to change; for now all we see are grandiose plans and words, words, words.

But it's best to return to reality: the office, the people that work there and the thrilling sensation that pushes you onward, even though you're not sure in which direction.

This is the air one breathes in America. It's an atmosphere in constant motion, where you're forced to seek out solutions. Details are worked out along the way.

Change means life.

On this subject, Alex recalled a Swedish friend who said to him one day, "In Sweden, the government makes one-tenth the number of decisions that the American government makes, over the same length of time. In

Sweden, we estimate that 80 percent of these decisions are right; while in America, only half are right. Translated into absolute figures, when in Sweden we make eight good calls a year, in America you make fifty. The advantage lies in the fact that in the U. S., when you realize you've made the wrong or the unfeasible or the unpopular decision, you're ready to renegotiate it then and there."

However, it must be admitted that the system is tough to grapple with and can even become a source of alienation. But all in all, it's a system that works, that produces civilization, well being and, above all, life.

This method is adopted when realizing a project. You can't expect perfection from the very beginning, otherwise you'd never even start. As you go along, you are allowed a margin of error, without going overboard. Decisions are re-adjusted, and together you strive for an acceptable solution. You are aware, though, that the product at hand is not the best possible, that it happens to meet a certain need at that particular time. And even before it is finished, you begin to think of the next project and how long it will take to realize, and how it will surely reflect the compromises of the project before it. In the meantime, the others are still grappling with the 320 problem of the first project, which still has not been completed.

This way of proceeding excited Alex and inspired the philosophy of his firm.

There he was, sitting at his work table in his office on the west coast of Florida, just a few hundred yards from the turquoise waters of the Gulf of Mexico and white sandy beaches. The door and windows were closed, the air conditioning was on – shutting out all familiar noises, the sun, and the desire to run along the beach or sail away and leave your cares and your anxiety-ridden relationship with humanity behind.

Concentration was a must. Without these continuous tests, life would go on like a sea of nothingness.

An unstoppable impulse obliges us to create problems for ourselves and others at work, in our more intimate sphere and, even in the simplest forms of communication.

Communicate, communicate, communicate.... But do we really want to communicate? It may be more precise to say we simply wish to transmit that which we consider opportune for the world and our kind to know. In us, the best and the worst of us is locked away, well protected – at times so well guarded that even we ourselves cannot decipher it.

It is thus that large and small problems are born.

False or interrupted communications whose aim is to set wider boundaries within which to work.

The main problem is that whoever starts this game must become convinced that he has expressed himself correctly. The initial rough going is forgotten, and so offense is taken should the interlocutor provide an interpretation that is perceived as distorted. The interlocutor, in turn, is alarmed and seeks out new ways, more "complex and subtle," around the obstacle.

Everything becomes more and more complicated.

The result is that positive intentions are set aside, along with reason and the serenity of the parties involved.

What a simple, silly process – yet at the same time it unleashes a whole series of destructive reactions!

How much intelligence and energy – mental, physical, chemical, atomic and so on – are wasted on trying to solve a simple communication problem!

It does seem almost like a game, yet it contains the deadly source of holocausts great and small – whether it is the holocaust of one or a thousand souls, of a single person or thousands of people, of a couple's relationship, of a business relationship, of a financial empire, of a religious belief, of a nation, of a people, and, who knows, maybe of the world itself, or a part of it. It's best to work, plan, live and not think too much.

Chapter 3

Towards noon Alex decided to take a few minutes for himself. He lifted the telephone receiver and dialed the number of his house in Colorado. His wife answered.

As he began to speak, he saw her as if she were right there in front of him. She looks very nice – an intelligent face, lively green eyes, blond hair, a slim build with warm, soft curves, long legs with round, full buttocks which, like her shoulders, have something sweet about them. She's nine years his junior. Like many women, she speaks passing from one subject to the next at the speed of light. It's great how they remember everything and, what's more, seem to control everything. It's truly a strange sensation!

As so often, he succumbed to his tendency to get mixed up, and could not completely follow her. He'd rather hear slower, more touching words, on subjects that give him time to relish her voice and lose himself in her embrace, albeit a long-distance one.

"Last night I went to dinner with Mary Kate and her husband. We talked a lot about this summer's Festival. You know, it's well-organized. But this year some of the concerts scheduled seem to be lacking in personality. There won't be many artists present – we'll miss having so many different ones and enjoying all the different interpretations. Some are downright mediocre. At the board meeting we said that last year's program was better. But despite our recommendations, they favored the economic aspect over the artistic. I think it's a mistake, and many people on the board agree with me. Too bad we couldn't convince the majority. It's the artistic content that's important, you always say…"

"Yes dear, I've always said that's the way to go and that you're right about it. But tell me, how are you doing? Enjoying the fresh mountain air? Our lovely little house with the fantastic view, the flowers? Are you happy? Would you like me to come up as soon as I can? Do you want to come back? Tell me about you, about us!"

"Of course, I miss you, I wish you were here. That's it – why don't you just hop on a plane and come?"

"In two days I have to be in South America, you know that!"

"Yes, but I think you let yourself get too busy, you're not able to organize your life and your travels in a humane way. You should reserve a little time for yourself. I'm sure you'd do the same things you've always done, and you'd have much more free time, a less hectic life, if only you knew how to get organized. Oh, the same old hard-head!"

"You're surely right, but my life is out of control, time's passing by too quickly, people want to talk to me, meet with me in order to make their decisions. It's either play the game all out, or it's best if you stop playing altogether. And you know I can't stop, at least for now. Maybe one day I'll learn. Come with me – it'll only be a six-day trip, maybe too short – but it'll be intense and beautiful."

"Oh sure, the usual six-day trip, with two nights spent on the plane! I already told you, you haven't got a clue when it comes to organizing your life."

"Then we can tack on another two days, and spend the weekend someplace nice."

"How can you even think such a thing? Like I'm really going to fly from Colorado to Florida and then to South America for a six-day vacation? Your head's in the clouds, mister! When are you going to grow up? You're like an 18-year-old!"

"Sorry, forget it. I've got an important call on another line. I'll call you tomorrow. Have fun, bye!"

When are you going to grow up?!

How many times had he heard that question repeated, and how many times had he responded, "Never!" And if he did grow up, where would all the creativity go, the simplicity, the desire to do things and keep up the fight, as if this all were some kind of giant circus? If he looked at the world the way the people at the country club did – who see life with grave eyes and a total lack of sense of humor – he'd rather be swallowed up by the sea and immediately be given the chance to see what lies beyond.

Somewhat disconcerted, between resignation and feeling sad, he took a stroll round the various computer stations.

He wanted to become immersed in concrete problems; he wanted to be useful, to use work as an escape, a form of distraction. An odd concept, it would seem – work as a means of distraction!

He walked, carrying his pencil with the large, soft point, the one that draws dark, easily visible marks.

Whatever the profession, the older one gets, the larger one's brush strokes can be.

The others still have to develop their own talent. They have to spend years in front of computer screens, following details, seeking out errors. They have to make neat, clear lists with sharp, finely tipped pens and pencils.

Some of them, Alex reflected, will spend their whole lives doing it. They have a thing for details.

For others it is a great sacrifice, part of a slow initiation process that will lead them to learn all they need to know in order to move on to a bigger canvas, or to create by scribbling away on the loose sheets of any old paper.

The whole process seems backward – you have to acquire a great deal of knowledge in order to become messy. Only at that point, your messes will be rife with ideas, solutions, experience, simplicity.

It's true, the key to the entire "world system" is finding a conceptually simple solution. The incredible thing is that this always exists, but it's so hard to see! It's so difficult that mankind will probably never have time enough to find all the possible solutions.

And that's why we thought up God. What a simple idea to explain everything!

And if we were God, or a portion thereof?

I imagine that one day we'll find out. And why not believe it? It's so beautiful an idea, it probably is true.

During this constructive exchange with his co-workers, he realized how he is ever more caught up in the intensity of his commitments.

Then everything must be proceeding as always.

When it comes down to it, life is just a big joke and he is deeply aware of this, because he is continually goaded by his sense of humor, which exposes his contradictions. But if you want the game to work, you've got to play seriously. This way, when someone asks him a question, he feels pushed to do his best to see that his answer is clear, satisfying and not evasive.

In short, a problem should be dealt with and solved in the best way possible at that particular point in time and space, making use of all the knowledge at our disposal.

When Alex does not feel sure of the solution, he takes his time. He returns to his office to think things over, to seek out information. He busies himself with telephone calls, reading, asking questions, reasoning, scribbling, writing, until he is ready to provide a reply which he, in good faith, feels is the best.

The effects of such an exhausting approach are felt in the evening, when, after dinner and a good bottle of wine, he collapses in an armchair and drifts off to sleep – unless there are friends over, with whom to exchange ideas.

If he sits in front of the television, it's all over: like swallowing enough sleeping pills to knock out a horse, the effect is immediate.

But that day, no matter how hard he tried to concentrate on work, he remained anxious. He felt the need to do something different. What, though?

Suddenly he was struck by the impelling desire for distraction. How?

"Let me give Pamela a call!"

It was about 6 p.m. in England, most likely she would still be at work. She distracted him. He found it hard to explain the feelings she inspired in him.

It was definitely not love, and not even passion.

Her deep voice activated a strange process in him, by which he was freed of earthly constraints.

It wasn't what she said. Perhaps she simply had the capacity to listen to him, and interrupt him at the right moment. Actually, this was an art.

Knowing when the other person is tired of listening to his own voice and continuing the verbal process.

At that point he'd be quite glad to be stopped by a word that distracted him, or a gesture of sweetness able to change the atmosphere. It's like being transported from one planet to another in a flash.

By himself, he's unable to do this.

By himself, he spends too much time going down the same road, over the same terrain, crushing the same blades of grass, until someone says to him simply, "Enough! Take a look at the sun!"

Pamela had this power.

She had dark hair, with hazel eyes, her skin a warm, almost amber color.

Her features were a bit hard, pleasant but not beautiful.

She was long and lean – perhaps too thin – with an excessively Anglo-Saxon posterior, though her two beautiful breasts compensated for this.

Who knows how much Anglo-Saxon blood actually ran through her veins?

At times she gave off a coastal Mediterranean scent, sunny and indolent, even if she acted with the boldness and self-assuredness typical of the women of Her Majesty, the Queen of England.

She was three years older than he, though her slim figure kept one from guessing her age.

When he spoke to her over the phone, he imagined her as a filly, pawing with her hooves, twisting and turning, then stomping with her front hooves and setting off into a trot round the corral, her head held high.

This was the most efficacious image to describe this lightly moving, crudely thinking woman, who at the same time was also profoundly sweet and tender, as one could read in her eyes.

They say the eyes are the windows to the soul. The soul of a filly is enchanted and open to the world, poised to filter new experiences through pupils that see objects magnified four times compared to human visual perception.

He called her office, no answer.

He called her cell phone.

Her voice seems to gush forth from a strange pathway, which runs from her lower belly to her throat as if by chance.

"I'm glad you called! It's great to hear from you."

"Where are you? What are you doing? Can you talk?"

"Yes, for a little bit. I'm on my way to an appointment, trying to make my way through this pandemonium of people and cars, in this city's bizarre climate – with weather that's hardly ever really nice and never really unbearable. I can't help but think how lucky you are with your beaches, the sea, the sun, and even real rain.

"In Florida, rain is truly an experience.

"It gives you the impression of being able to nourish yourself with the sheer downpour, of being able to hug those dark or white clouds that move quickly and threateningly to block out the sun.

"Here, it just rains.

"Sometimes you can't tell whether the drops come from above you or below. But I have to admit, there's something romantic about it, something that makes you want to cuddle up with somebody and...dream."

Alex responded, "Always the optimist! You see the positive side of everything!" and thought that this woman was just what the doctor ordered for his soul, his mind. He didn't know why, but she sparked his fantasy and the world became much more receptive.

He did, though, feel foolish for having uttered such a phrase, about her seeing "the positive side of everything." It was already such an obvious aspect of her character, and they had known each other for too long.

"What do you say?" he continued. "You want to go to where the sun is? Wouldn't you like a nice trip to a hot place? Nothing extraordinary, mind you, but we can make it extraordinary if we want to, if we convince ourselves!"

"But I'm up to my ears, at home and at work. My son's away at college, but my teenage daughter's still home, with typical teenage problems. No big deal but you get the picture – she needs me. Besides that, I have a whole list of appointments to..."

"Just plan everything out. I'll work around your schedule."

He smiled to himself, as he considered his ability in organizing his travels – short trips though they were.

"I have to go to Brazil for an industrial design project. I'll send you a plane ticket so we can meet. I'll be in Rio for two days, then Sao Paolo and vicinity. Or I could go to Sao Paolo first, by myself, while you stay in Rio and relax. We can meet there. And when my business is over, we can take off for a couple days together, who knows, to Bahia maybe. Doesn't that sound like a great trip? Leave the rain and the traffic behind for the sun, sea and sand. True, it might still be crowded, but...»

"Let me think about it. I've just reached my appointment. I'll talk to you tomorrow. Call me! Bye! I have to admit – I'm dying to be with you, have you pick my brain. See you soon, sweet thing!"

True, he was sweet inside and every so often he longed to share this sweetness.

Just being together, watching the people go by, the unfolding of nature's activities, the flight of birds, the crashing of the waves as they rise and die upon the beach, the evolution of the cars that wind in and out of traffic.

Looking in order to feel like outsiders, observers – detached, yet involved in one's own emotions, in the pleasure of feeling close, of touching or merely brushing up against one another.

Chapter 4

How pleasant it is to relax aboard a plane after so much hurrying, pushing and shoving, waiting, taxi rides, goodbyes, questions, telephone calls, last-minute decisions.

You close the door on work, on your responsibilities, on having to pack your bags, on having to leave messages....

You're on the plane, the hum of the engines lulls you to sleep. At last, a seat all your own, big or small that it may be, depending on what class you're flying – but a seat all your own.

You're in someone else's hands, you might as well relax and convince yourself that they know what they're doing. You cannot intervene. Just let destiny run its course.

Or forget about destiny altogether, and think – whatever happens, pleasant or unpleasant, you'll wake up in another reality, in a different city, with different customs, amid people who are different from the ones you left behind. The weather will probably be different, too. If worse comes to worst, you'll wake up in a completely different world.

Sleep and dream.

Drink your wine and get drunk on your thoughts.

You can think whatever you wish, your life is literally suspended in midair.

Exchanges with your world have been interrupted and you must absolutely keep them as such, even if you happen to have a telephone at your disposal, which is watching you from the back of the seat in front of you, or whose presence you can feel under the armrest of your seat.

Using that phone would only mean honing that sensation of impotence, because no matter what news may be communicated to you or any question that you may be asked, you, in that moment, cannot move or act. The only concrete result you'd get out of it would be anxiety and agitation.

You might as well let yourself be rocked by the impalpability of the air, the buzzing of the engines, and postpone all action till after arrival.

It's like reaching the top of a mountain and forgetting how hard the climb was. You catch your breath and begin to think of the descent and the warm fireplace you'll be relaxing in front of that evening. They're different moments in life!

Let the world turn without you – it's going to turn anyway. Let "your destiny" turn around you, undisturbed.

Now you've left behind the almost dramatic race in the car to get there on time, the struggle against the traffic plotting to make you miss your flight. And the orders left to your co-workers, the fear that you forgot something as you reviewed the documents.

This is the daily routine of a person dedicated to his or her job in this day and age.

I'm sure it has always been this way, though. It's just that, in the past, people took longer breaks. There were different means of transportation, there was more time to think.

When you got to a new place and made contact with the new reality, you couldn't just fax or email information or ask for a confirmation of something you'd forgotten.

You were really alone, you didn't know if everything was okay at home, whether your affairs were prospering or not, not even whether your country was at peace or at war.

When you acted, you had to leave many possibilities open, as you waited for the next ship or stagecoach to come in, carrying news that was already days or even months old.

Life may have been more arduous back then, and the theory that the major cause of stress today is the speed at which we're forced to act is merely the result of an all-too-superficial analysis conducted by contemporary man to justify our weakness.

What is certain is that we cannot ask our predecessors for any clues here, and we have not been able to figure out all that much from their writings.

He thought of these things while considering a book he had brought with him on the plane, which presented a very modern approach to interpreting the arrival of the Spanish in the New World. The book described – or better, interpreted – the relationships between the

Conquistadors and the natives, and the wars and cruelty that followed.

The facts were recounted in a somewhat distorted fashion, through the eyes of someone born and raised during the current historical phase of western culture, where the main parameter for comparison is the concept of democratization. For some strange reason, we feel responsible for the atrocities our ancestors committed as they imposed their way of living and thinking.

What's more, we feel responsible for the mere fact that they even tried to impose their convictions, about whose intrinsic worth we ourselves harbor serious doubts.

There was something a priori in this judgment, the unbending will to lacerate one's own spirit, to fill with guilt one's own status as a white man, who apparently dominates the scene today.

Alex was struck by the fact that the author of the book made no attempt whatsoever to see things the way people saw them during the epoch in question. What we today consider gratuitous cruelty was then actually part of the system. Cruelty was a common practice used by both sides. It was a way of thinking and acting, typical of men who had to create an impression of being resolute and "courageous."

Almost always, the perpetrators of such cruelty did not have to fear public opinion. They would make use of the best means possible to report the news in a version most advantageous to their purposes.

Without the existence of radio, television, telephone, news could not be reported as it happened, events could not be commented on as they unfolded.

There existed only "God," created by the men of both civilizations, who either approved or disapproved of men's actions.

And as this God was not identical for the two contending sides, he either punished or rewarded on the basis of criteria that were thoroughly irreconcilable.

And it may not be said that this mechanism has faded from use, even now. On the contrary, it's more alive at the present time in history than ever. It's just that today it is lived and manipulated in a different manner.

Writing about the past with the mentality of today, without making an effort to understand the reality and peculiarities of a different age, is almost a sacrilege. It's tantamount to wanting to create a third God to judge the other two, and to justify this act by saying our God is more democratic.

Alex thought about whether these reflections made any sense or not, if even the adjective "democratic" actually referred to something concrete, something definable. More likely, it represented the umpteenth historical justification that made it possible to manipulate the world from a different position. Perhaps it was only the revenge on the part of a once defeated God.

In any case, it was all too complicated!

The humming of the engines put him to sleep.

After several announcements, the routine on board changed. There was movement about, everyone was doing something, getting ready.

After a night spent hoping dawn would come quickly, it was time to prepare for landing. It was time to think about going through that series of bothersome, unvarying motions – drag your carry-on, ride the escalator, wait in line, show your passport, wait for your baggage hoping it hasn't been lost, lug it through customs, a medieval throw-back complete with duties and taxes and needless bureaucracy. You have to ask yourself, in a world where the order of the day is "globalization," should this ritual be taken seriously or as a game set up to render the tourist's life less monotonous? Lastly, there's the trip from the airport to your final destination. I say trip, because usually it is much more difficult and complicated than your flight across the ocean.

At the end of this whole process await either new encounters or your return home, which, if it isn't easier, at least gives you the impression that you've concluded something. In the latter scenario, a new chapter begins, you're re-immersed in the old routine, which just then actually seems exciting. Only tomorrow will everything become once again humdrum – you resume your habits, as wonderful or as pernicious, as amusing or boring as they may be. The sensation of being different, an outsider, the feeling of exhaustion, justified by your long journey, vanishes, dissolved by the reality that absorbs you.

The airplane is landing in London, from Rio de Janeiro. Indeed, Alex had gone to Brazil by himself to do business.

Brazil was a lovely country where life is good, despite the many complex social and economic problems. People there want to live, and live with gusto. It appears they have no time to despise one another, the way it happens in many other Latin American countries.

There's something extraordinary, indefinable in the women there, which is also hard to find in other places. Alex knew this well. He was accustomed to it.

But at that time, Alex stood in need of affection with deep roots in an old relationship – one in which words were superfluous, and where the tricks of the game of love had been used up and forgotten long ago.

That's why he had stepped up his work and taken a plane to London. If she couldn't come to him, he would go to her.

He even had an excuse if his dedicated workingman's spirit acted up – he could take advantage of this visit to Europe to arrange some business meetings that he had put off for too long. Though the more he thought about it, the flimsier that excuse appeared.

All he could see were two deep, intense eyes waiting for him at the airport.

Just a few more minutes!

A smile, their hands clasp, their cheeks brush up against one another's, a "Hi, how've you been?"

Nothing more – and the whole scene seemed to be played out in slow motion, as if to test the intensity of an encounter that both of them longed for.

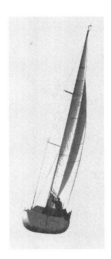

Chapter 5

The dull light of the late London afternoon was slowly dying out, and so was the intensity of the glow diffused throughout his hotel suite. What a difference compared to the quick but intense Florida sunsets!

One minute, the red solar disk is dropping before your very eyes, the next, there's an almost sudden flash and an insistent twilight that seems to emerge from the gray of the ocean and project itself towards the sky.

Everything becomes monochromatic, except when the moon returns to revive the chiaroscuro of the waves, the branches of the trees, the outlines of objects.

He called his office to let them know where he could be reached. He couldn't completely avoid the rat race of his life.

These were only life's stolen moments, but they were life itself!

And what moments they were!

He abandoned the window and shifted his attention towards the bedroom, which was separated from the living area, where the telephone was, by a very English-looking wooden portal. He fixed his concentration on an image that provoked in him a pleasant sensation, but at the same time brought on a feeling of unease in the center of his chest, which seemed to descend into his gut. She was lying on her side, her naked back visible, her legs covered by the sheet.

That white, rumpled up cloth protected her amber body, highlighting the wide curve which rapidly swooped down toward her waist. One could guess the form of her hips through the sheets.

Her back was bent slightly forward, leaving the base of her left breast uncovered – perhaps to shield her eyes from the light, she held her arm over her face. That arm was pressed against her hair, which lay spread over the pillow, black and wavy.

At that moment she was a Venus, though he knew full well that she was not one of those super shapely, incredibly beautiful women. But sex doesn't necessarily have anything to do with beauty. Sex follows different paths for everyone, its ways are hard to assess and comprehend.

He had to admit that this woman possessed some sort of invisible third hand, which rummaged inside his stomach, his bowels, his brain. Luckily, their encounters were always brief, though they were regular. To spend a semi-vacation together, keeping work to the bare minimum – seeking one another out, touching, enjoying relaxed conversation, detached from the rest of the world, a meeting-clashing of minds. Then each would once again feel ready to face life, pretty much oblivious to the electricity unleashed during those few days spent together.

What good fortune!

It was like a strong wind sweeping along the horizon and racing on its way. It carries the boat as it blows. It fills you with enthusiasm and tempers your spirit, but then it must move on – while it lets you relish the beautiful day it has brought in its wake.

That was the first afternoon he'd spent with her after his transatlantic night flight. The wind would not be dying down for a while yet.

There were too many things to say, do and explore together.

After hanging up the phone he slipped back beneath the triangle of sheets that covered her legs. He felt relaxed and supple, as if his was the body of a teenager. The torpor and tension in his muscles from the plane ride had by now vanished.

He placed the palm of his hand on her belly and pulled her toward him so that her back and thighs clung to his body without admitting the slightest opening or gap.

She offered no resistance and delicately slipped into the new position. She was probably not even completely awake.

Her warmth filled his insides and surely even his soul, and he grew drowsy, imagining how later they would go for dinner in a nice restaurant, and that before going to sleep they would make love once again, slow and easy, with passion and thought.

The next day they would go shopping, visit museums and, who knows, maybe even the zoo, like two kids in love with life.

He surely did not care to remember that this would be their only full night spent together during this trip.

In fact, the next night, around midnight, Pamela would have to be off, like Cinderella – back home to her children, whom she would tell who knows what lies to justify her two days' absence, time she had spent trying to communicate in a dimension outside the daily routine.

Some call it love, others sex, still others call it sin or betrayal.

It would be much simpler to consider it for what it actually is – a mutual, innocent exchange of imagination and energy, something that reassures us that we are the product of the fusion of body and soul, both of which require regular maintenance.

Chapter 6

Alex spent four days in London. Four beautiful days. He'd arranged several extremely profitable meetings, but most of all, he experienced that excitement in his gut that he had known in high school back in Italy, and later at college in the United States.

He would count the remaining hours left to study, before he would be free to see his girlfriend again.

It was almost a physical pain to bear, an annoyance.

He'd thought this was "kid stuff." And yet he rediscovered with satisfaction how that day in London, even while he was concentrating on his work, every now and then his thoughts would race to the appointment he had later that afternoon with Pamela.

He made plans, thought about which restaurant to take her to, reflected as to whether it would be better to organize something or to simply give themselves up to spending time together, living and breathing – not that the air in London was particularly healthy, though this seemed like an insignificant detail.

They discussed traveling, the sea, the mountains, green fields and sails unfurled in the wind – and the air around them became purified, colored with pink sunsets and transparent lights.

A few days later he understood that that excitement really was "kid stuff" – because that excitement is what kids are all about. Their lives are based on it.

He was already off in another country – Italy – dealing with other problems, meeting with different people.

He found himself calling Colorado time and time again.

Pamela was back to her daily routine – work, the kids. She did, however, invite an old friend home, who lived not far from her and made for interesting company.

Yes, that excitement in the stomach would, for the moment, be forgotten. It might come back again, true, but one had to admit that it was much different from the excitement of youth. There was something dull, almost thought out, about it, as if created unconsciously to whisk one away from the stress of daily life.

After all, they were only looking for the awareness of being alive, the acknowledgement of sharing something whose importance they could both guess.

But they could not fully grasp the concept that lay behind the pleasure of knowing that the other existed and that his or her presence could become real and tangible thanks to regular encounters, even if they were diluted over time.

And strangely enough, their appointments did resemble youthful encounters, while at the same time they left ample space for the unfolding of their own lives and the intertwining of other relationships, which curiously were just as intense.

How truly multiform life is!

Why, then, did humanity tend to pigeonhole life by trying to turn wonderful and horrible moments into choices that must be made definitive, or nearly so?

All it took was a careful look around to realize that at the bottom of it all lies the vulnerability of existence, which is something like a great mass of water traversed by unpredictable currents.

Above, the winds of evolution blow without letting up, in an attempt to lend meaning to the waves; various methods are tried, which seem completely new, but in reality they are but a repetition, in a slightly different form, of a system which dominates the entire universe, man included.

Perhaps evolution is not the right term. It's just an on-going perturbation, like the effect of wind on water.

It's better to let life run through you and distribute enthusiasm where it may, without crystallizing behavior and anointing with a sacrament something that is destined to change.

In truth, giving and receiving are separated by an almost imperceptible line, so fine we can barely make it out. For instance, it is commonly thought that a gift brings more pleasure to the person giving it than to the person on the receiving end.

Indeed, the receiver may not even like the object that has been given to him or her, and what's more, must now devise some way of returning the favor.

The giver, at any rate, is gratified by the act of giving.

Alex recalled how in London he hugged Pamela and did not know exactly what to say. Each phrase could have broken the fragile equilibrium of the moment, or create embarrassment once the feeling had passed.

Then, practically with tears in his eyes, he whispered to her, "You're special," without being sure it was the right thing to say.

"Stop right where you are. Forget other words. Don't try to say things that are bigger than you are. You're special to me, too, I like being with you, you convey your sun-bathed intensity to me. But please, let's not go beyond that."

As she spoke she looked at him with her shadowy, velvety eyes, which seemed to be saying, "I'm thinking of something else, I've got lots of different problems in my life to deal with. You can do only so much to help me, and you mustn't upset the balance that I have struggled to attain after a broken marriage and another relationship ruined by pettiness. Women are not the 'fair sex.' That definition is most likely connected to physical strength. You just can't push things too much and constantly put your own spiritual resilience to the test. Women naturally create an initial mental defense – it's deeply ingrained within us."

He understood.

He also understood that he had no right to enter the most sacred part of her self, where the human being seeks shelter to relish and assimilate emotions that may be beautiful or ugly, important or superficial, transitory or definitive.

But can there be definitive emotions? He asked her this in a whisper, and heard her soothing, distant reply.

"I don't know, maybe death, but I doubt it."

Chapter 7

Location: the usual business lunch with seven people in a restaurant in a typical Italian village perched on a hilltop some 100 kilometers north of Rome. The subject at hand: the design of objects for production at a local factory, and rationalization of each single project to lower costs of production.

In truth, there was very little that was "usual" about that lunch.

In Italian hill towns, which still smack of the Middle Ages or the Renaissance, even a simple lunch can be a unique experience. Sitting round the table with your dining companions, you get a feeling of completeness and gratification, although you're not quite sure whether it's the food or the very atmosphere itself.

One thing is for certain – this sensation accompanies you along the narrow streets and in the various places you visit.

As is the custom, the conversation takes a turn toward other topics just before coffee arrives.

Back in the office after lunch there will be time to study in detail the problems that still must be worked out, and pinpoint things that were only discussed in general terms around the table. But for now, the dishes must still be cleared away, glasses are still full of wine – and as often happens in such situations, Italians talk politics.

Throughout his years of globetrotting, he had never been in a country where people were as passionate about politics as Italians. People would discuss everyone and everything in politics at the drop of a hat, if only for the pleasure of complaining, boasting, offending someone, considering themselves better than anyone else on this planet, bemoaning their situation… and then everything would go on as before, unchanged.

He was convinced that Italy was a solid oligarchy based on the concept of the "violin that is held in the left and played with the right."

Only right and left are not actual political convictions, but simple labels invented to best exploit the system.

Given that the Italians have always been considered "virtuosi," in the sense that they know how to do difficult things, perhaps the violin has only a single string. Paganini showed the world that you can finish a concert for violin with a single string.

What's more, these hands have become so skilled and practiced that they no longer require the participation of the rest of the body. Both muscle structures and intellect become superfluous. Only two hands with five fingers each are necessary, nothing more.

A superb meeting of theory and practice, whittled down to one string and ten fingers. The rest of the body is free to move, follow, sway, but it will always be just a spectator. It's like a violinist dressed in black, playing his instrument in the dark, his white hands in a spotlight.

The body – the nation – takes no part in the show.

An evocative image: the violin, the government, the hands and the fingers of the oligarchy. A dialogue carried out on a string between two white hands that approach and distance themselves from one another depending on the notes and the position of the bow – the two hands never touch or separate altogether, otherwise the concert would be over.

A prodigious invention.

An oligarchy justified by music, art, creativity, intellect. And what an uproar there would be should the program ever change!

Unfortunately, the result is boring, monotonous repetition.

But if you only attend the show sporadically, this little spectacle can indeed be entertaining.

The two snow-white hands move about in order to quell the murmuring of the audience – which at times may be bored or attentive or passive, but fundamentally gratified.

If it weren't, the murmuring would grow and eventually interrupt the performance.

These two hands – their fingers, veins, muscles, nerves, joints and skin – must feel important. What a great dream they live out, even if it is ignored by the rest of the world, unknown to anyone outside the audience!

Alex considered how far many new, emerging countries were from such perverse sophistication.

These people with a long history and ancient spirit have been re-awakened by modern economic-demographic prodding. These young nations, some with old, recycled names, others with names so new they're difficult to remember, still employ direct intimidation; their sole weapon, a strong political party, religion or bonds of kinship. In the end, the result is the same, but for worldwide public opinion the system is too unrefined and hard to digest.

They have passed from the Middle Ages to the modern epoch without having honed themselves and their system, without attaining sophistication and so-called "modernity" where the masses are assigned their own form of importance.

It's like a big, new game. It works if played well, and if the survival of the system is guaranteed.

Not wars or violence, but philosophy, secret abuses, frustration distributed by bureaucratic machines and crusades to solve secondary problems which to the general public are of utmost importance. Serious topics are discussed behind closed doors, by the usual crew in charge – people with the ability to maintain their position of power indefinitely.

How odd!

More than 2,000 years ago the Romans and their "Romanness" delineated a very clear concept of the "republic," which is to say, the confrontation of ideas and powers.

For them it was like a virus that kept coming back. No one, not even the great Julius Caesar, was completely exempt – indeed, he, too, was destroyed by it.

The virus multiplied; strains became contaminated through the upheaval of invasions, migrations, revolutions, restorations, compromises and intransigence.

But a tiny patch remained unblemished, in one of the most remote of Roman colonies, Britannia.

A group of these men's descendents, still under the effects of this virus, had landed on the North American continent, bringing with them the very same symbols – eagles, fasces (bundles of rods containing an ax with a blade projecting, proud emblems of power displayed in the U.S. Senate), columns, obelisks, rotundas, large arenas, city streets laid out in grid fashion, homes with patios and swimming pools, and so on.

Along with these symbols came similar lifestyles and ways of coping with problems.

As with the ancient legions, from the beginning the ranks of their armies were filled with colonists, men willing to put up with a temporary sacrifice in order to one day be able to return to work "their" land in "freedom."

Along this route, the evolution of a great nation would not be far off – and the Founding Fathers of the United States of America knew it.

Surely, even today, a large portion of American citizens has no idea of where their roots lie – how, in reality, they are the spitting image of *cives romanus* when it comes to dealing with the rest of the world. Yes, it's a more up-to-date version, because the times change – but the vices and virtues are similar. With Rome came legions, lawyers, laws, the mobility of their armies in defense of their interests and *pax romana*. There was the ongoing quest for a better life for its citizens, freedom of religion, separation of Church and State, the diffusion of its language, lifestyle and approach to problem-solving.

Unfortunately, with time, this well-oiled machine underwent massive infiltrations.

Perhaps those who most exploited it were the Christians.

Where else could they have found a better mechanism to aid in their spread?

Too bad that in using this machine, they broke it.

Alex caught himself thinking that perhaps today the United States of America was moving dangerously far from the Founding Fathers' concepts.

Who knows what will eventually be responsible for breaking the system?

Perhaps admitting the existence of the word "stress," which was unknown in America as late as World War II, launched the process of weakening.

The second step was its increasingly dangerous interest in the rivalry between those who must assume responsibility for concrete actions and those who merely criticize and obtain personal advantage.

In the past, one was allowed to improvise. It was okay to make mistakes, as long as one strove to do his best.

The law was a serious thing, work was a serious thing. The many tricks to extort money like it was going out of style had not been invented yet.

The mass media didn't have to go looking for occurrences of little importance and blow them up until they became nagging international news items.

Newspapers and television networks today must be gorged with information – too many programs, pages and stress for the people who have to satisfy the hunger for news, build audiences and bring home a positive financial return.

These thoughts made Alex's heart wrench.

He was an American; he believed in America.

But really, the United States was only now beginning to have to deal with the first signs of weakness. The road was still long. No doubt there would be myriad opportunities to recover, considering the mobility of the system.

Even ancient Rome went through harrowing periods of highs and lows.

Returning to Europe, and especially to Italy, and in particular to those same seven hills of Rome where it had all begun, one could perceive that the contaminated portion of that old virus had in some way remained there latent.

Toward the end of the second millennium, Alex had come across a pathetic puppet show, right *there*, on the same ancient hills that had spread throughout the world the great concept of a "true" democratic republic.

This concept is difficult and must not be confused with the more simplistic, populist concept of democracy.

In the democratic republic, the person or persons elected make decisions and take responsibility for the consequences. They may not hide between what we today call polls or twisted party logic. The people in charge must lead the nation for the period that is their term of office, and risk being substituted should they fail in their duties; and in any case, they return to being normal citizens once their term has expired.

But today, upon those very same hills, Alex found a new ludicrous republic based on a mixed up conception of democracy, which sails along now colliding into the right shore, now smacking into the left, down a river of words that is constantly overflowing its banks.

And as one observes this reality, a question arises spontaneously: Will these newly-formed nations which are now experiencing their Renaissance at the speed of light, and possessed of the unconfessed desire to achieve institutional structures similar to those of the United States, succeed in their aims?

Won't it be easier to succumb to the temptation of taking a much shorter step – that is, stopping at mid-river and letting themselves be dragged along by the flow of words?

As Alex sipped a classic shot of after-dinner liquor, he was struck by a feeling of discomfort. It dawned on him that he would have to spend the entire afternoon, plus another full day, immersed in such a reality.

He had ceased to listen to the discussion. He was overcome by great sadness for the beautiful land of Italy. He wondered how Italy would ever survive the madness that consumed her, that robbed her of her energy, her passion and her capital. For many years now he had not been a part of that system. He knew he was powerless and could never fully understand the language of his native land.

Oh, how distant lay his dear friend Florida!

That afternoon, when they discussed in greater detail problems regarding work and dealing with the competition, he realized that most Italian industries either belonged to huge multinational corporations or had transferred their activities abroad, retaining only an Italian image.

There were only two alternatives to this reality – become simple suppliers for large companies or close. The economic strength of Italy, which is to say small and medium-sized industries, had been under attack for too long. In fact, a whole array of commercial interests had been targeted.

He had the feeling that this state of things could, after al, actually represent a solution for the *Bel Paese*. That ridiculous political-bureaucratic system controlled by those funny little politicians would never again strike fear in the hearts of the great multinationals, and some kind of practical agreement would have to be reached in order to save the economy from ruin – even if it did turn out to be less advantageous.

Rationalization of the system would come in through the side door – through the economy – a very important door nonetheless.

People have to live, eat, work, move, enjoy themselves, and the government exists solely to make sure all of this is possible. It should have no job other than making the citizen's life easier and more pleasant.

Thus, the economy that runs the world will, without realizing it, help Italians get back in touch with themselves and free themselves from this oligarchy.

His heart ached and he recalled Alessandro Manzoni's epic poem, *Adelchi*:

Return to your majestic ruins,
To your peacetime job in the shop that burns,
To the drenched furrows of the servant sweat.
The strong blends in with the enemy defeated,
Alongside the new master the old one is seated,
Both people are now atop the hill,
Slaves they share, livestock too;
They lie together on the fields so cruel
Of a long lost peasant whose name is nil.

He consoled himself – these were different times, today the watchword for planet Earth was globalization. And tomorrow he would catch a plane for home.

Chapter 8

Another flight. This time, Rome – New York. Alex had an appointment with his wife, who at that moment must have been on the plane from Colorado. He thought of her with great emotion and nostalgia.

In truth, it wasn't his wife that would be hugging him once he got to New York, but Margareth, his soul mate – with blond hair, green eyes and a quick wit. Forever Margareth, his one and only, just as he had courted her so many years ago.

He could file all his work problems, for the time being, somewhere in the back of his brain. He enjoyed imagining the pleasure he would receive from this encounter.

Based on past experiences, he knew that seeing her would be like opening the shutters upon a magnificent florid garden, warmed by the late spring sun. He also knew that it would be a short-lived sensation.

In the room that was now lit by this bright new light, which had chased away the dimness, there would soon come bees, gnats, hornets, mosquitoes and wasps. The joyful explosion of colors in the garden would be followed by an annoyance that would wipe out the afternoon's peace inside the cool room in the country home.

At any rate, his spirit was attracted by her presence, by the vision of her, her proximity, more than by her beauty, which even so was remarkable.

He always sought her out during and after his flights and wanderings in the name of work, solitude, passion. In her scent, he detected her powerful influence over him, which constrained him to give to her all that he could – love, protection, financial security, attention – to make her feel happy and free.

When she was ill, he went so far as to wish he could take her place – but never would he give up his whole life for her, for his freedom was another thing altogether.

She had been his one and only wife, and he had no intention of having another. She was perhaps the only thing truly steady in his life, and theirs was surely what is commonly called "true love."

He often experienced this wonderful sensation – when their time would come to leave this world, their feelings for one another would without a doubt have kept them united. At that crucial moment they would think, soon we shall meet again. The one who passed on first would do everything possible to communicate with his or her living partner. They had prepared phrases containing a message or imagery, in the hopes of somehow transmitting them. Their spirits were very much united, they would find a way to communicate.

All true, true, true.

His whole being vibrated when he thought of her – sometimes positively, other times with anger – whatever the case, it vibrated.

And when it came down to it, his life revolved around the two of them, their sweet moments of intimacy, and their clashes as well, which now and again led them to exchange harsh words.

But he could not, would not give up all his freedom of living for her. He had to protect his freedom to go off by himself sometimes, to flee and then return; to take great business risks, and even to enjoy the intimacy of another individual so that he might better understand what nature has in store for him and others, grasp more of nature's secrets.

And the same went for Margareth. Alex loved her and longed for her own happiness to evolve, that she might fill herself up with experiences and sensations. He hoped she would find the time to discover and live out her own intimate sphere by herself, and that she would also share this with others, and discover new continually intersecting pathways. Who knows how often this happens, and we don't even realize it.

He reflected on how much alike they were, though the ways they expressed themselves were very different.

They certainly enriched one another's experience by taking such different routes, ways that had so little in common, as they relished moments, situations and intimacies that were altogether different.

Someone had made sure that the nature of men and women, their goals, were rife with distinct nuances, so that life would be interesting and meaningful for those living it.

Alex realized how difficult it was to harmonize this conception of life with the rules and regulations of present-day society.

There had to be a way to explain that helping yourself or someone else to be free is an act of love. Of course, this freedom must not hinder the other's freedom, nor should it offend to the point of no return the feelings and dignity of the other, which should go hand-in-hand with the right to be women and men.

In truth, these lacerations are mostly caused by erroneous teachings that inject into our blood a sort of potent drug which exalts jealousy and hate. These lacerations feed deep rifts among opinions and beliefs, creating feelings of guilt over perfectly natural behavior.

The saddest and most degrading aspect is that these opinions or beliefs seek to prevail by shouting out their morals to the world – morals that are all too often superficial, abstruse and uncouth.

No one, however, is completely immune to the effects of this drug, and life becomes complicated.

Let's return to our peaceful room in the country, overlooking the garden in full bloom. It's now swarming with extremely bothersome flies and hornets.

But they need to eat, too, and fly around and land and do all those things that they normally do. It's their life. If you want to enjoy the sunshine and take in the beauty of the flowers, you've got to put up with the presence of insects.

The relationship between husband and wife was the same. She needed an outlet, a way to utilize her dialectical intelligence to test her influence over him, and so on.

In return, they illuminated one another with their company. The important thing was to be aware of it, and most of all to remember that this intense game had a well defined limit in terms of time.

All one had to do was to close the shutters, but not all the way, leaving just a tiny strip of light shining through.

The flowers relished the sun's joy – but outside.

And the bugs attracted by the light could fly out through the open space.

While he savored his thoughts in the dim of the room, one bond remained: that band of light and the certainty that later, the call of that garden would automatically push him to open the window back up.

And the game would start all over again.

He wondered if by explaining to the world the sense of such human needs, and by using a simple story like this, people would understand; or would they just smile and slough it off as an idiotic opinion?

Whatever the world thought, he was determined in his credo. He could neither give to anyone else all his earthly life, all his freedom, nor could he ask it of them.

The most intimate part of the soul, maybe.

But our actions, our lives belong to us and only to us.

Chapter 9

They had arranged to meet in New York, in a pleasant hotel suite which they also used whenever they had business meetings in the city.

They had kept a small apartment there for years, but in the end decided that using a hotel was simpler and more comfortable. Actually, they went to New York less and less often now, and for shorter stays.

With the passing of the years, the sun, the sea, the mountains attracted them much more.

And New York, although very interesting, was just a city.

He took a taxi from the airport to the hotel. It's always nice to walk into a place where people know you by name and greet you with a smile.

The concierge handed him his key and said, "Your wife has already arrived. She's waiting for you in your suite."

She was watching TV. He entered and saw only her blond hair, which cascaded upon her shoulders.

She turned around.

Affection, love, memories shared, the intense sweetness of her green eyes, the vitality within his spirit, the joy of seeing one another again, and many, many other things all added up, transformed that meeting into a collision of tensions – a desire to pick each other's brains, and at the same time a longing for tenderness.

But there would be two days of truce, during which life's doubts and tensions would retreat into the shadows.

They would leave room for the certainty, if short-lived, that nothing could change the sensation of mutual gratification in the rhythm of life, as if nothing to the contrary had ever happened or would ever happen.

Only afterward, suddenly, would they realize they were two people, alive and different.

Then the scene would change. The old curtain that hides the scenery would be raised, and habits, memories, passions would win out, like a mass of water that can no longer be held back.

And this, when it came down to it, was a good thing.

A positive spark that shoots from the daily routine, which forces us to forget ourselves, so that we become more intimately united with the human herd.

The herd exists and we are part of it, but inside we are individuals. We live alone with our problems, confrontations, suffering, separation, rancor, alliances, hostility, hate; as we do with closeness, love, deep friendships, generosity, altruism…and more problems, confrontations…and so on.

Truly childish!

Deep down inside, almost all of us are just kids dressed as adults.

The farce of life, if it were to be observed by an extraterrestrial, would appear to be a monotonous repetition of situations that were always the same, easily understood – just complicated by the fact that there are so many different actors. And all of it aimed at attaining a pleasant feeling of personal gratification and the knowledge that you're somebody.

Grand illusions!

In reality, the mechanism is so simple that at times it seems squalid, and admitting it would mean the total destruction of our egos. What's worse, afterward we wouldn't have any more fun playing the game of life.

Following these two days of truce, Alex began to recognize in Margareth the changes in her behavior which had become more deeply rooted in recent years, and which were responsible for continuous friction between them.

This time he'd decided to get to the bottom of the problem and find an explanation, or better, a strategy for dealing with it.

He knew he'd be entering into that labyrinth where many questions about life are asked, and where one tends to forget that we are all part of the "world" system. Indeed, all of us feel the same pain, satisfaction, experience the same undoings and victories.

Margareth had always been a difficult woman, who deep down felt sure she was acting for the well-being of her man and her family. At the same time, she was so involved in her own existence that she diffused around her a sense of impalpable, almost princely egoism.

She seemed impregnated with the spirit of an ancient sovereign, whom everyone and everything were obliged to appease.

And strangely enough, people did try to appease her, even complete strangers.

Yet, she also knew how to take care of the people who helped her with disarming simplicity; at times with just a smile she would give to them exactly what they desired at that moment. She did this with grace, enveloped with ancient magnanimity.

He had always lived beside her, loving her with the awareness of her unconscious vision of life.

He participated in this shifting balance – from a cheerful, girlish nature that was intelligent and carefree in dealing with the problems of existence, to the ancient spirit that ruled the depths of her personality.

Unfortunately, for the past three years or so, this mechanism seemed to have gotten stuck.

Anyone who knew the woman well could see this easily enough.

For his part, Alex was sure of it.

The causes for this change could have been many. She was still pleasantly beautiful, but not the stunningly gorgeous girl she once was; the kids were by now off to college, and though they spent hours talking on the phone with her, they no longer gave her maternal satisfaction; a few minor health problems; the reduced elasticity of her body, an ache here, a pain there which one learns to live with as the years go by, to the point where if you stop feeling them you begin to wonder whether you're still alive; her change of role, from young woman participating in the anxiety-ridden, disorderly life of her husband to self-assured matron ever more involved in her social commitments.

This could have been the main cause of that distortion. It was as if she had turned a page on her almost rebel existence of days gone by, bursting with new experiences and passions shared with her man.

But perhaps the page had not been turned all the way. Margareth often returned to take a peek at the previous chapter.

He began to consider her friends one by one. Some of them he admired. There was one in particular, who was quite an elderly lady, but possessed of a sharp mind and a heart still able to love, give and receive.

Others were on the surface more complex, but inside they were fragile.

Who could tell what influence they had on her mood?

Some had already gone through one or two marriages and were still looking for love that their limited theories on freedom and independence for women would have destroyed in a matter of days. They didn't realize that it's practically impossible to be profoundly independent and free without reaching compromises with nature and other people, both men and women.

He had reached the point where he hoped his wife had taken a so-called lover, or had a friend she could spend intense, or even just light and carefree hours with, perhaps reading poetry under a tree together.

He had also discovered, as he rummaged about his own feelings, that romantic poetry readings beneath a tree created a sort of "competitive jealousy" in him.

He and his wife understood one another's deepest souls. What, then, could be deeper than fully sharing in the intensity of a poem?

Although finding a decent companion for everything else might have been the solution.

One day Margareth told him that she'd been seeing a psychologist – a woman psychologist – for some time.

This too must have had a certain impact on her. Alex began to understand the source of some of Margareth's more recent utterances, which had so little to do with her way of being a woman. For instance, "You have to solve the problem within yourself – don't dump it on me."

Alex explained he had no particular problem with what they happened to be discussing at that moment, and he hardly thought she was upset by something so serious that she wanted to project it onto him.

It was but an observation of little importance, that she had inserted into the conversation. And yet as insignificant a topic as it was, it grew and grew in emotional intensity until it finally exploded into an argument, though both of them forgot how it had begun.

She had never been a stubborn woman, nor had he ever been a stubborn man. It was for this that they always managed to find a way around every stumbling block and hardship. Lately, though, the process had grown more and more difficult, distressing.

Alex began to suspect that the psychologist was behind this negative trend.

The human brain is like a highly complex power plant.

He had read that if we had the ability to control the connections of our brain circuits for just a few seconds for each connection, the operation would require hundreds of years to complete. Imagine how long it would take to understand the entire brain!

The only thing possible for the moment was to catalog from the outside the reactions of individuals, and note the common answers which were linked to similar developmental patterns – or intervene with chemical support, depending on what the doctors say.

The observations should lead to the right path for the patient, along which he or she may proceed with conviction, even if one risks becoming more vexed than before, if the same obstacles are run up against.

The patient has taken the route indicated by science, and accuses the others of acting inappropriately, selfishly – thus unloading his or her own frustrations on them.

Where does the problem lie?

The pathways are only similar in appearance, and the solutions are too personal.

Could this have been one of the reasons for the changes in his wife?

The zealous psychologist, after many years of study and sacrifice, was using a system that was too logical – she had failed to understand Margareth's true personality. Thus, she had undermined that brilliant union that was such an integral part of her self – an ancient spirit with the heart of a young girl, enveloped in the beautiful body of a woman.

Alex interrupted his thoughts – as Margareth had left the bedroom smiling and amused.

She wore a simple but very pretty dress, with various shades of blue. She loved colors and knew how to use them.

"How about going out for a nice dinner, Mr. Alex Mancini!"

Once again, the storm had passed. That evening they could be young and simple again.

Tomorrow…

The next day, they decided to go to the Egyptian section of the Metropolitan Museum. The sky was clear. On the stairs of the museum there were many people; they all seemed quite at ease and happy. Up and down they went, meeting one another, talking as if they were part of the building's soul, part of the city's. Different accents, skin colors, ways of dressing all mixing.

This was the spirit of America.

Alex saw it move among the skyscrapers, rush over great stretches of trees, deserts, plains, country, lakes and mountains.

It wound its way through Central Park to reacquire self-awareness, then took off again, wrapping round new skyscrapers, dispersing itself amid forests, deserts, plains, country, lakes and mountains.

It washed over the shores and went wandering through the world, making a vast swath, and in the end returned to the same beaches, and once again through forests, deserts, plains, country, lakes and mountains. And of course, punctually back to the skyscrapers of the big cities and the more modest constructions in the small ones.

To breathe in America is like absorbing a bit of its spirit.

And the people on the stairs were doing just that.

As they walked toward the museum entrance, Margareth and Alex both thought the same thing – how those around them as well were experiencing the pleasantness of movement and life, a sensation which might not follow them inside the museum once they'd reached the top of the stairs. "Museum" conjures up images of a dead world, one that has already been lived, the past. And yet the objects on display were laid out so as to convey a living historical message.

One had the impression that the centuries of ancient Egypt were unfolding there, right before your very eyes, in room after room, with clarity.

Even in a context such as this, practicality and the obsession for research oozed forth. Contemporary America sought to find similarities between itself and ancient Egypt. The common air of creativity was palpable. There was a desire to evolve, organize, plan, fend off attacks by tired and negative ideas, create.

The most important element was the perception that the two civilizations were certain of making history.

They were joined by their aim to plot, safeguard and dominate the origins of their prosperity.

The origin of one: the waters of the Nile and its precious lifeblood so well administered.

The origin of the other: the regeneration of nature, a broad-ranging search to control the resources of the earth and perhaps of the entire universe.

Great dimensions, grandiose ideas – in proportion to the technology and sources of energy available during the two different historical periods.

As the two made their way through the museum, observing statues and objects, they tried to identify themselves with the representations of these ancient ancestors and the things they made.

They wandered and realized that with the passing of time they could relate more and more to the ancient Egyptian world. The statues were no longer statues of people that lived thousands of years ago, but Alex and Margareth – living in two different eras, breathing two different breezes composed of the same kind of air.

They held hands like two school kids, transmitting to one another their emotions and feeling the same shivers along their spines – an ancient instant. That is, an instant with respect to the centuries that bridged the world in which we physically inhabit today and the one in which, in that particular circumstance, we believe we have lived.

At the exit they found themselves embracing, rubbing their cheeks together, as if to feel alive and still united in that splendid late morning, lit up by the same sun that was once called Ammon.

The next day Alex boarded a plane back to Florida, to work. Margareth headed back to Colorado, to the thousand commitments that a woman on vacation is able to contrive.

Part Two

Chapter 10

The boat was anchored in the lagoon. There was hardly any wind. Alex looked at the stars. The waters of the Gulf of Mexico wedged their way through the strait, bringing with them a vast wealth that lapped against the shores of the continent and the islands that delineated the lagoon.

At that moment the current created by a robust incoming tide was strong. It flowed along the hull, emitting an almost constant rushing sound. It looked as though the bow were moving with respect to the water, with the mast shifting, now toward south, now toward north, as it stood out against the black background of the sky, which appeared to be held up by many screws with light-up heads – the stars.

In the mirror of water that surrounded the boat, one could perceive continuous movements: tiny splashes, vibrations, calls.

From deep within the hull came a crackling sound that revealed the existence of an underwater life.

Amid all this agitation, Alex felt relaxed, anchored and steady. His senses were awakened, poised to detect any nuance of life. He sipped a glass of wine, accompanied by a few cookies.

"The old-timers from the hills of Piedmont in Italy were right," he thought, "when they said in the dialect of their noble wine-producing land, 'Una stisa e un grissin.'" Translated, with a somewhat free interpretation, it meant that wine should be drunk in small doses, and always accompanied by something solid.

Wise words, indeed!

Drinking without eating makes you drunk, burns your stomach, makes it impossible to appreciate a wine's roundness and bouquet.

The mouth should be slowly cleansed, the acidity absorbed. Then, always with a certain deliberation, another sip is taken.

Such a theory was well suited to the surrounding scene – the slow, barely perceptible rocking of the boat, the rush of the water, the stars, fish, the presence of nature in general, the tension of the chain that held the anchor, which guaranteed that this night's sleep would be peaceful.

Slowly, sip after sip, cookie after cookie, all around became harmonized and melted into a single sensation.

It seemed as if the world were no longer in a hurry.

It was a timeless scene.

How many sailing vessels must have dropped anchor on those protected waters! Vessels big and small, simple row boats, motorboats, yachts…

Now, that was a new word: motor!

Then came another: "radio," and a third: "television," and the fourth: "telephone," and the fifth: "GPS," and the sixth: "radar," and so on. This hodgepodge of names came to Alex's mind in no logical sequence.

Then he thought how of he had all those objects on his sailboat – sometimes even two of the same item, so as always to have a spare on hand.

His boat was beautiful, well-equipped and fast.

He reflected on the pleasure derived from owning such a boat.

It had cost a pretty penny, but still, it was something well within the reach of many people. In the past, it probably would have been a luxury that only kings, princes and other powerful men could afford. Today there were thousands of such boats sailing the seas – now, there was another great novelty!

Behind this reality, though, lay a huge mechanism called production – frantic activity based on capital, suppliers, labor, engineers, marketing. It was a system that worked only if assiduously managed and monitored.

The fancying of these thoughts while anchored so calmly, peacefully, seemed to materialize in one word which today was much abused: stress.

Yet another word invented by our age.

Just like the star atop a Christmas tree. Only, this tree was composed of a confused jumble of computers, telephones, airplanes, wheels, turbines, pistons, engine blocks, propellers…

Stress – was not that word the symbol of our times?

We use it and abuse it to justify all sorts of behavior. And perhaps we get a certain kick out of using it.

But is it really our invention, or have we but found a new name for one of humanity's old companions, weakness?

After all, stress is the same as weakness, which is the same as a flagging spirit, a lack of that fortitude which was so important back in the days of Republican Rome.

Was fortitude the buzzword back then, the way stress is today?

He had often asked himself this question, and he was never able to come up with an adequate response.

He knew only that he could leave that lagoon whenever he pleased, without having to make too many compromises with the elements of nature.

He had an electric windlass to weigh anchor, an engine that could drive the boat against the current until he'd found a favorable wind, GPS, radar and echo sounder which guided his boat through darkness of the thickest fog.

Had it always been so easy?

Perhaps the real fear is that, from one moment to the next, all of this just stops.

We're running on a treadmill which remains stationary. The more we accelerate, the more we realize that the whole thing might come to a brusque stop any second. The faster the belt beneath our feet turns, the worse our fall is going to be if the machine suddenly breaks.

Perhaps the problem of stress is just this.

But if you do fall, the tension may just disappear altogether once you're lying on the ground.

You'll have to deal with other problems, on another level. You'll have to focus on how to get up, on how to repair the damage to your body, on how to move, eat, sleep, go to the bathroom, and so on.

Now, though, while the treadmill's still going, you're just afraid.

But why was he thinking all these thoughts?

Why did he watch the stars and feel dissatisfied?

The stars were up there; he was down here.

So what?

Everything was in working order – the engine, the sails, the instruments, the food, the wine, his wife, his relationships, his profession, his children – one of whom worked with him, while the other was in New York at a firm affiliated with his own.

They were two smart kids, full of enthusiasm, very close to him and his wife.

The stars were there above him.

They were all above him, shining a deep, distant light.

What was it about them that attracted him? And the sea gurgling against his boat, what was it about it that attracted him?

He was happy, at least on the surface.

A few years ago he began to paint, delegating more responsibility to his children.

Plus, after years of working with the same people, together they had created a highly functional organization.

Now he felt all but useless, and perhaps somewhat bored.

He really felt the need to paint.

And what strange paintings he created, very expressive.

They took from nature its colors and shapes, and transmitted a message of fluidity, which seemed to wander on seas of light and stellar tones.

He began painting three years ago. Six years ago he had made his last business trip to Italy, outside Rome.

Practically, nothing had changed, just that he had eliminated Italy from his business travel itinerary. Too much time wasted.

Now he would go only to walk those history-steeped streets, to delight in the ruins of as yet unsurpassed Roman glory, which today's Italy has nothing in common with. He roamed about the old ruins, he lived in the past, ate and drank to nourish the present.

Why do the stars sway?

Why do they twinkle?

Why was his soul no longer aboard a safe, well-equipped boat?

Why did his job seem to belong to others?

Why did he view his paintings as a joke, too easy to paint?

Then there's mankind in general – best not to think of it.

Was it worth making sacrifices for the people who worked with him?

Yes.

Even the supreme sacrifice of giving up peace of mind?

This he did not know.

Margareth and Pamela were both important for that spark of life they knew how to provide; what did they communicate to him?

Margareth, the love and companion of his life; Pamela, a friend during his flights from routine, his sidekick for great adventures in the body of a woman.

It was 4 in the morning.

His whole world spun around him, not just the stars.

He awoke his dozing sailor and said, "Let's go home."

The wind was weak, the stars were high, the anchor weighed. The boat began to move.

The light of dawn caught them by surprise, on the open sea.

The breeze blew softly, but it was enough to push the boat along at a reasonable speed.

Perhaps six knots, maybe only five. He had no desire to check his instruments. They bored him.

He was at sea.

Suddenly he was struck by a thought, no sure if it were profound or idiotic – what color is the wind?

He remembered how in Lugano one day he had met a curious painter who confessed to him that it was his obsession to paint the color of the wind.

At the time, Alex had given it little thought beause it turned out that the painter was making his living as a bank employee.

But then he thought it over. Never underestimate anybody.

Now he was at sea, observing the recurring miracle of the rising of the sun as a gentle breeze barely riffled the surface.

The tone of the sky was going from blue to azure to gray, finally reaching the color of egg yolk mixed with the white.

Not red, not orange, but pale and alluring, inspiring sleep and calm.

It was all there, painted before him.

The only thing missing was the color of the breeze, which later in the course of the day would certainly become the color of the wind.

He tried to forget about all this. He dozed off, then awoke because the boat was leaning too much to one side. The automatic pilot was set to keep on course, but it could not take into account the direction of the wind.

He sat on the bridge. He noticed that the wind had suddenly whipped up, changing directions somewhat.

His assistant looked at him, waiting to hear an order – adjust the course and head more into the wind or ease the sails?

A few minutes passed. Alex said nothing.

The other grew more and more anxious.

Alex heard these words come out of his mouth – "Do you know the color of the wind?"

Long-lasting silence, a little embarrassment.

Then he said, "Ease the sails – let me just enjoy this moment in peace."

Tomorrow it's back to the office.

But he did not report to work the next day.

He stayed home to think and paint. He was irritated. Even if everything were okay, he was irritated.

He looked out the window, observed the sky and the water in the lagoon behind his house.

The wind was very light. It was a magnificent day. No one had called him from the office yet, but he felt irritated all the same.

His vivid imagination, which had always been there, was now abandoning him.

He couldn't imagine the color of the wind.

Perhaps it was too deep a question, or too foolish a question. Or, as with all great scientific discoveries, the exact answer was within reach, though it seemed more hidden each day.

Would this be a discovery that rocked the world, or just a passing piece of trivia?

Perhaps he should retreat for a while, to a dimension of life that could draw him closer to the universe, like when Jesus went off into the desert. But his desert was the sea, and he wasn't Jesus. At this point he ceased to even believe he was normal.

Jesus wasn't normal either, and he had different concerns. He said many things, but he never showed us the color of the wind.

"Maybe it's up to me to find the color of the wind – me, and me alone. My mission. If my desert is the sea, I'll empty the boat of everything I don't need. I'll take the bare necessities with me, and I'll wander about the sea. I'll wander until I discover the color of the wind."

Chapter 11

The people he worked with began to look at him suspiciously. They could no longer understand him. Before, it was so easy to interpret his eagerness, his victories, his difficult moments.

His children were concerned, and they telephoned one another in search of an explanation.

Margareth was the most philosophical.

She knew him well, had faith in him. She knew that at the right moment his peculiarities would vanish and in their place leave a man who was ready to cope with reality. This time, however, she had to admit that she couldn't figure out why he was behaving in such a way. It seemed as though something was gnawing at him from within, which he did not want to admit. This had happened before, but he had always found an outlet in his work.

Pamela lived very far away, and during their regular but infrequent meetings, was accustomed to dealing with his apprehensions.

She adored him, but knew also that he was not "her man." He was a friend who came and went. He gave her advice about her work, but could not always be there to protect her and share in her moods.

Certain nuances were beyond her grasp.

He kept saying he wanted to take a year off and go sailing alone.

Strange, he wasn't a big fan of sailing by himself. He liked going with a few good people, or even if it was just his assistant.

He liked to fill his boat with bottles of wine and tasty foods, and talk of bays where they could anchor and take part in the local life.

He was as curious as Ulysses.

Only this time it was different.

He wanted to bring along minimal provisions, with just a few bottles of wine, only for special occasions. And most of all, he wanted to be alone, with no real destination in mind.

Those close to him did all they could to convince him not to go, appealing to his sense of openness toward the world, family, friends, co-workers, consultants.

But no one had ever imagined that Alex was out to discover the color of the wind.

One afternoon he left.

Two days later his wife received a letter in which he explained the reasons for his departure. He wrote that she could show the letter to anyone she wanted.

The kids were assailed by doubts, but they had so much faith in their father that, despite their surprise, they refrained from comment.

Other friends thought he was mad. The people at work figured something was up, though they didn't know what.

Only Margareth did not lose heart.

Yes, she was concerned – after all, he was out there all by himself. But she knew that he was sensing the scent of the sea, and this comforted her. If the universe ever allowed him to return, he'd become the most perfect man she had ever known – otherwise, she'd meet him in another life.

Pamela received a short letter a few days later.

She was perplexed.

She lay down and thought for a while about why Alex was so tormented by that stupid obsession over the color of the wind. It must have been, she imagined, that he sought an explanation for his relationship with the world through nature.

She wouldn't mind putting up with a little seasickness herself, if it could lead to an answer of that kind. But she had no time for such things, no opportunity. She could only hope that he would share his emotions with her once he returned, if he returned.

Margareth, on the other hand, knew exactly what she would say to him. She was only waiting for Alex to share his emotions with her.

If he never returned, she would try to recognize, in some way, the magic word they'd agreed on to let the other know that he or she had departed from this world. A word that could clear up certain doubts which are very common among mortals.

They did not know how to communicate this word yet, but they surely would find a way.

He was riding the sea in his sailboat, headed south-southwest. He could still see the west coast of Florida behind him.

In a few days' time he had reached the Caribbean Sea, where he sailed aimlessly. He had no hurry, he wasn't going anywhere. He spent a few hours each day fishing, ate somewhat-stale food, drank as little as possible, gathered rain water. He had a little GPS aboard, which gave him his location, but he'd promised himself to use it only rarely, just to confirm his position.

He wanted to sail as sailors once did, making do with his old sextant, which he barely remembered how to use.

He'd get better at it.

His goal, however, was not the same as the sailors of old. They sought out new lands, while he sought to stay clear of dry land, inasmuch as his own strength and store of provisions permitted. He would have even circled the same sea over and over again to avoid setting foot on land.

He did have one great advantage over his predecessors – he could rely on his automatic pilot, which performed the work of at least three persons, keeping the boat on course night and day.

Actually, he had two automatic pilots.

One was a real automatic pilot, which used a complex electronic system to hold a pre-plotted course. There was only one problem with it. It consumed a lot of energy, sometimes more than the solar panels and the wind-powered generator could furnish. Thus, it was to be used only rarely.

The other was a so-called self-steering system, which, with its rudder connected to a wind blade, kept the angle of the boat at a constant with respect to the direction of the wind.

The route could vary, depending on which direction the wind came from, but this mattered little to Alex. He referred to them both as automatic pilots, even if this was not exactly the correct terminology, and even though the two devices basically performed different tasks. He had named them Riccardo senior and Riccardo junior, respectively.

That name was inspired by an old Milanese folk song, which told of the life at a tavern on the outskirts of town. At one point, it went like this: "Luckily we have Riccardo, who plays pool by himself. He's no great company, but he's the nicest guy around!" For Alex, those two Riccardos were indeed a boon, even though they did not keep him company.

After a few days, it occurred to Alex that the Pacific Ocean was bigger.

There he would find the solitude he was after, and would embark upon a more intense relationship with the sea.

The big obstacle was crossing the Panama Canal.

He detested bureaucracy of any kind and sought to go ashore as little as possible – which always meant the tedious filling out of forms, answering questions which were always the same, hearing himself called captain and his beloved boat called a vessel or a ship, depending on where he was and the language used.

It was an invasion of the intimacy for the both. They had nothing to do with any of that. They were literally following the wind to learn its secret.

It would have been much easier if they'd just left Alex and his boat alone, just as Alex and his boat left them alone. For Alex and his boat, all that mattered was the sea and the wind.

He thought a lot about whether to undergo the sacrifice of lining up at the canal entrance, waiting his turn, having to deal with ship pilots and officials.

Yes, the sacrifice would be worth it.

It would lead him straight to the great Pacific Ocean, and perhaps he would return only by way of Cape Horn.

This didn't matter. He wouldn't think about his return, and besides, he wasn't in search of daring feats and seas. All he wanted to do was wander the ocean and observe the wind.

He crossed the Panama Canal, and where he headed we'll never know, because he really couldn't have cared.

He learned to talk very much to himself.

He made up brilliant conversations.

Then he went a step further. He began talking to the birds and dolphins that he met, and that followed him. He was sure they understood basically what he was saying, and it seemed to him that he could understand their answers.

It took a long time, a very long time, to reach this point.

Most of all, though, he learned to communicate with the clouds and storms. He came to realize that they aimed to treat him fairly well. And the more he spoke with them, the more he beseeched them to help him – for instance, to tell him which way to turn in order to steer clear of a strong squall on the horizon – the more it seemed to him that they did provide the right indications.

The wind was the only one he couldn't manage to communicate with.

It came from afar and then went on its way. When it was too light, he asked it to pick up at least four or five knots to fill the sails and move them along.

When it was too strong he begged it to diminish its vehemence, because it had tired him out.

But the wind never listened to him!

He thought, "It comes from too far away. It takes note of me only as it passes by, but then it's already gone, leaving nothing behind it, not even a colored streak."

There are zones with a mix of colors in the wind, but they are not the wind's colors. All the wind could do was caress them, polish the sky, the sun, the moon or the sea, bringing out these surreal tones.

"I have to remember what they look like. If I ever return, I could paint them."

He often caught himself saying "If I ever return."

He considered this a weakness, since he was supposed to be focusing solely on the present, communicating only with the things and beings around him. But human nature is weak – it takes a long time to become familiar with new customs.

He leisurely recalled how back in Florida he'd set out for a short trip, even for just three days at a time, and would fill that boat up with an amazing quantity of delicacies. There would be enough supplies for a month. And plenty of wine!

He would say that he never knew who he might meet – if he ran into friends on their boats he could invite them on board to talk and eat and drink together.

If he happened to find no one, he'd eat and drink more himself, between bouts of sailing and anchoring.

Now his aim was to see as few people as possible. He sought to survive by forgetting and learning anew.

Back in Florida the trick was to get away from work and enjoy nature for a few days, forgetting about the stress.

It wasn't necessary to learn anything new – the idea was just to caress the joys of nature.

Here in the middle of the ocean, sometimes these joys became torments, fears which raised many questions – how to survive, how to rest, how to feed oneself?

Apart from these fundamental differences, the routine was very similar, but repeated day in, day out until they wore you out.

Then he would come home to his pool in the backyard, which he would jump right into after every sailing adventure. It freshened him up, like new. He would splash around in the fresh water at length, letting it penetrate his body and cleanse it of the salt that had been deposited there.

Sometimes now he would do the same thing, when it rained hard and long. This, of course, depended on the atmospheric conditions, and not on an object that was always there at his disposal like a swimming pool.

There were times when it didn't rain for days on end, and this was awful. And when it rained during a squall, he had to keep his mind on the boat. It was annoying how everything became so slippery that it complicated every movement.

At times it rained when you had no desire to get wet, perhaps while you were sleeping peacefully in the cockpit.

Sometimes the rain came softly and sweetly, just at the right time. When this happened it was a cause for celebration, because it happened so rarely. But then, it might last so long as to become absurd.

Diving in, swimming in the pool. Getting out when you wanted and taking a shower. Having a cocktail and then going to dinner. These were memories of the past.

And they seemed so distant.

He wondered whether all of that had ever really existed. Were they dreams or reality?

After these brief relapses, he would set himself back to work with gusto.

Then he remembered how before he used to work much more and the burden he was under. Which was better?

In life there are no perfectly defined situations, just compromises.

He had always believed in this principle, and part of setting out on his own had been to check the truth of this theory.

The color of the wind had to be a well defined thing.

When it blew hard, it would allow no compromises – the same as the sea, squalls, storms.

Instead he was slowly discovering that perhaps they, too, had no exact understanding of the logic behind their functioning.

Surely, he had to seek out compromises with all of them. He had to raise or lower the sails, change course in order to position the boat as securely as possible amid the waves, sleep when he could, wash when he got the chance.

At the same time, though, he could in some way control these factors and make use of the sea, the water and the wind – pretty much when he fancied. But they would let themselves be managed only up to a certain point.

It was like always, like everyday life. Up to what point did the two sides have to assert their will to compromise, in order that both survive? Then existence on a mountain or at sea was not so different.

Maybe the wind had many colors, many different shades of colors, or worse yet – maybe it was colorless in order not to compromise itself, so it could always slip away without a trace of its misdeeds or assistance granted.

It just polishes existing colors, makes us see them in another light, transparent, without a fixed tonality.

All that changed was the intensity of the message, which is gone with the wind.

This was just a theory. It still needed to be proven.

* * *

Every now and then he needed peace and rest.

He had to take time out to abandon his obsession of sailing on, sailing on, sailing on…

He would look for a quiet place to drop anchor, and stop. He slept, relaxed, thought. He thought very intensely. When he was well anchored he didn't have anything else to do.

Sometimes he went ashore and talked to a few people, exchanged a few opinions. But then he felt the need to return to his boat.

These stops could be a big problem. If there were a town or city nearby and they spotted his boat, he would have to go through all those stupid formalities that make men in uniform feel so important.

Sometimes he would get it over with as soon as he had dropped anchor. Other times he would take a chance, and if no one had come for him in a couple days, he would weigh anchor and be off. He knew that this could get him into some nettlesome problems, but the impulse to avoid the bother of having to show his papers to the authorities was stronger than he was.

This was one of those days.

He had decided to drop anchor behind a promontory that offered protection from the prevailing winds.

It wasn't an actual promontory, as it was not very high, though it was prominent with respect to the rest of the bay and the beach along the coast.

He couldn't tell to what extent the height was due to the elevation of the land or the luxurious, compact vegetation.

His anchor hit bottom at about sundown. The hour when sailors' hearts are filled with tenderness.

He enjoyed sleeping like a log.

He felt like he was back in the Florida lagoons, in spring or fall, when the breeze rocks you, the boat rocks you, and you sleep, sleep, sleep.

You feel you can pierce the sky with your dreams.

He thoroughly relaxed. He sorely needed a rest.

The sun appeared in the sky and began its climb.

Gradually the light became brighter, and his longing for sleep became greater as well. He did it almost unconsciously, half-closing his eyes in his bed, which he found extremely comfortable and, strangely enough, almost completely motionless.

The sun rose to its daily zenith, high and bright. He could catch a glimpse of it through the open hatches.

He felt lazier all the time, and at the same time he could hear the memories of his life in Florida knocking softly at his heart. He thought, "I mustn't open the door to these calls. I don't know with certainty the answers to my old questions. I feel that they are maturing, but then again I ask myself whether I'll be convinced of their truthfulness."

Strange!

A disorderly splashing of water, whose sound recalled no animal's, had reached his ears.

It was right outside his berth, near the hull.

With a certain reluctance, he decided to get up and go see what it was.

He was very curious!

He stuck his head out the companion way with great caution. He wanted to take part in what was happening without interfering.

For a few seconds he remained dumbfounded. He rubbed his eyes, so he could be sure of what he saw. He lowered his head, then re-emerged from the companion way, just long enough to get a better grasp of what was going on.

He looked around. His was the only boat anchored in that place.

Of course, the place was not to be considered all that protected, though to him it was like a dream. The boat rocked softly, compared to the nights spent on the ocean.

There were two sailboats anchored further toward shore, behind a second strip of land.

He could see their masts.

And judging from those masts, they must have been large, majestic vessels.

But they were quite far off.

Nearby was the cause of the lapping sounds he had heard – a tiny inflatable with a woman, who must have been about 35, and a young man of no more than 19 or 20, on board.

She sat crouching in the bow, her gaze turned toward the horizon, while her companion sat astern, his feet dangling in the water.

In reality, the inflatable looked more like an oval donut, without bow or stern, but the woman, who was slender and almost immobile, reminded him of a figurehead, and the boy a kind of human outboard motor that pushed the boat along ever so slowly.

Where had they come from? What were they doing out there? She contemplated the horizon as if inspired, the boy stared at the ripples the movement of his feet produced.

It could have been a scene near any beach. But to Alex, who had come in from the high seas and was anchored still quite far from all human activity, it was like a vision.

Ah, maybe he'd been a recluse for too long!

It had been a while since he'd seen other human beings, and these two were particularly beautiful. They gave the impression of possessing great inner vitality.

Perhaps this was his own desire for excitement after having spent the night quietly anchored. The only way to find out was to communicate with them.

Chapter 12

Only when he held out his hand to help the young woman up the ladder, which he had just lowered from his boat, did he take note of the uniform coloring of her skin, a delicate tan that brought to mind the adjective "warm." What's more, she was completely nude.

The boy handed her a bag, grabbed another and brought it with him, as he too climbed aboard, ebullient, holding the line attached to their inflatable.

She was smiling, more with her eyes than with her mouth, and when he touched her arm as he accompanied her to the cockpit, he learned how appropriate the adjective "warm" really was.

Once sitting down in the cockpit, she opened her bag and put on a blouse that reached to her thighs.

The boy, who had lively, attentive eyes, tied the inflatable to the stern and skipped over to sit down as well, in a position that allowed the sun to dry him and his skimpy swimsuit.

"Can I offer you something to drink? I could make something to eat. First, let's have a drink, then we can catch some fresh fish and cook it up. I've had a long trip, I haven't got much in the way of supplies."

The boy watched the young woman, showing great interest in the plan. She did not reply, but was looking around, as if trying to familiarize herself with Alex's boat – so the boy spoke up. He had a kind of mix between a British accent and New England speech. "I'll catch us a fish, give me fifteen minutes. And I'd love something to drink."

"Adam, you always reply a little too quickly for my taste. I was trying to figure out why we're on this boat, with this gentleman. There's something strange about all this, but nice. I can't quite put my finger on it."

She paused, then said, as if waking from a dream, "It's fine with me. Can I lend a hand? I'm Sophie. I don't know how to explain this, but I'm really enjoying being here in this cockpit. I'm feeling positive vibrations. I feel very calm and at ease."

He was a bit taken aback.

What was the meaning of all this?

Here was someone who seemed extremely receptive and sensitive, who just showed up from who knows where, and who after just a few minutes of conversation was uttering such an unusual and so propitious a phrase… *I feel very calm and at ease.*

"My name is Alex," he replied, "I feel pretty mellow today myself. That's all right, Sophie – I'll go and see what I have to drink, and Adam will catch us a nice fish. You stay where you are. I don't know what I have left. Too bad I don't have anything cold. But I have three more bottles of wine, for special occasions. And today seems like a pretty special occasion to me."

"We can drink wine later. I'd like some water for now, and I believe so would Adam – isn't that right?"

Adam agreed.

The two got to work, one going down to the galley in search of water, and the other setting about catching fish.

Sophie walked about the deck, now gazing at the horizon, now looking back at the shore, now taking in the details of the boat. It seemed as if her gaze caressed objects as a way of impressing them upon her memory, and her nose sniffed in the air to make it her own.

Alex observed her as he set the table he had brought up to the cockpit.

She returned to reality, came over to him and said, "Your boat is very pleasant, but now let me help you. I can't just sit around without doing anything, off in a dream world, while the others are doing all the work. We should work together, and dream together – or each take turns in a more organized fashion. Isn't that the way things work on board?"

She laughed as she said this to him, revealing brilliant white teeth, two dimples on her cheeks and a soft but determined air about her.

He passed her three glasses of water.

She placed two on the table, and brought the third to the young fellow fishing from the stern with a line taken from his bag and bait from a bucket that in the meantime he'd retrieved from the inflatable.

It looked like a typical boat-life scene – him, her, the boy.

An outside observer would only have had a little difficulty in figuring out the relationships among the three of them. One would never have imagined that all this was due simply to a fortuitous encounter – they appeared to be so harmoniously meshed.

They behaved as if they had come out for a day of sailing and would be moored only long enough to enjoy the sunset.

They opened the bottle of wine.

They spoke little and eyed one another with interest. The fish was good and cooked with great care – Alex was down to the last of his propane gas for cooking.

Sophie had an elastic body and moved with remarkable nimbleness.

Her brown hair practically blended in with her tanned skin. She had green eyes, a wide forehead, soft, somewhat rounded features.

She was not very tall, but had long, well sculpted legs which harmonized nicely with her hips and the curve of her waist. She had two good-sized breasts which hung quite naturally and were a part of her – no cosmetic surgery.

What struck him most was the brightness of her eyes, her face, and oddly enough, her uniformly tanned skin.

She said she was born in Massachusetts – of an American father and French mother.

She did not mention what she was doing in that part of the sea, or what she did in life. She didn't talk about herself. She talked about the sea, beaches, birds, the sun, the breeze, the wind.

When she spoke of the wind whipping up at sea, or blowing the trees, she seemed to get excited.

How odd!

She often repeated the noun "serenity" and the adjective "spiritual."

She said serenity could be achieved by nourishing the spirit within us. Only, she never explained what she meant by "spirit within us."

She spoke in vague terms, smiled a lot, as if she were testing the waters.

Adam was dark-hued, with messy, but not long hair. His eyes were dark and deep, but not very big. He had sharp features.

His gaze was intense and revealed great cheerfulness and a lively mind.

He thought like an adult. He controlled his impulses and his words; he expressed deep concepts and made interesting observations.

He asked very specific questions about the boat and Alex's travels, and listened to the answers with interest.

Alex was glad that both were possessed of sensitive souls and very polite manners.

How was it that they had met at sea, off a coast that was pretty much uninhabited?

It seemed as if they had known one another for years!

Who had sent them?

He had the feeling that this was no chance encounter.

After lunch and a bit of wine – the first he'd eaten and drunk like that in quite a while – he felt like he was back in Florida, along with a young helper and a friend who helped to ease his solitude.

Had his solo flight perhaps come to an end?

Had he returned to normal life?

Had he at last found what he was looking for or had he given up his search?

There was, however, something odd about the whole thing. Maybe it was the off taste of the wine, due to the heat or the rocking of the waves.

He had the distinct sensation that this was not an ordinary situation.

He knew nothing of the land that lay astern.

He knew nothing of that strangely matched couple. He could not figure out the relationship between the two of them and could not understand the relationship that he himself had with her.

The whole thing was steeped in incomprehensible sensations that were good for the heart and eyes.

No, he was still looking for an answer – and he felt certain that someone had come along to share in that search.

Had that strange couple been sent from the sky?

All three of them fell asleep outside – he and Sophie in the cockpit, the boy on the forward deck, where he had gone to check on some odd movement in the water.

He really loved to fish!

Astern, one could hear the splashing of the inflatable on its line. A quarter of the moon shone, while scads of stars dotted the sky.

For Alex, that night went by very slowly.

He soon fell into a deep sleep, as it had been a while since he had enjoyed such a nice meal and tasted wine – the beverage which up until this trip had been an essential part of his daily diet.

He awoke some two hours later.

Perhaps this was because that morning he had slept until late; perhaps it was also due to the presence of these two human beings who had broken the on-board rhythm and inspired new questions and new sensations.

It may also have been that supple body curled up on the other seat in the cockpit, from which a strangely familiar warmth emanated – perhaps just the fact that it was a woman's warmth.

Now and again Sophie would shift into a more comfortable position, revealing different anatomical particulars, each one perfectly tan and inviting.

It was 2 a.m.

He got up and took a walk around the deck.

The boy slept on his side, upon a thin little mattress that Alex had given him. The kid dozed peacefully, semi-covered by a coat.

The wind was distant.

The sea watched over them with its immense power, at that moment sleepy and serene.

He went down to the cabin to get three light blankets. He had a good number of them, on account of how wet they would get. He loved sleeping with a dry blanket.

He put one on the boy, who rolled over and seemed to appreciate it. He did the same with Sophie. He brought his pillow from the cockpit to a flat area toward the stern. He stretched out beneath the remaining blanket, his mind set on falling back to sleep.

It was damp.

Once again, he found himself counting the stars. He thought of nothing. Perhaps it was a new way of sleeping with your eyes open.

On his boat he had experimented with many different ways of sleeping, including sleeping while at the helm.

He would wake up only that instant necessary to correct the rudder when he heard the sails flap or felt the boat leaning too much to one side. It would be just a second, he turned the wheel to adjust the course and immediately fell back to sleep as if he had never woken up in the first place.

The automatic pilot was surely better, but it did have its drawbacks and could not always be relied upon.

At any rate, now he felt as if he were sleeping.

It was very peaceful; he felt in good company, he had no desire to think of anything else.

He slept without dreaming, yet he seemed to see the stars. Perhaps he was simply dreaming that he was sleeping beneath the stars.

He was very perplexed about what he was doing, and yet when it came down to it, he really didn't care.

If he woke up, all it meant was that he would sleep more tomorrow. He didn't have to go to work, didn't have to sail, didn't have to think. He just had to wait until the wind found him.

While in this undefined mood he felt a rustling, followed by a more resolute movement. Sophie had gotten up and brought her pillow and blanket over to Alex, and lay down there beside him. She lifted his blanket and snuggled up close. She fell back to sleep as if this were the most natural thing in the world.

In truth, it was the most natural thing in the world!

People were created to live together.

He had been the one trying to get away from them, and not the other way around.

Chapter 13

The sun was high in the sky, its daily arc nearly halfway completed. There was a light, steady wind. The sea had become somewhat rough.

The boat left a clean wake in its path, heading north.

They'd left the mooring behind the promontory more than 24 hours ago.

Life on board had become extremely pleasant. He was embarrassed to have to admit it.

He'd wasted so much time wearing himself down all alone at sea. He felt much older than when he'd set out, and he had the sensation that his appearance had aged as a consequence.

Sophie bathed with sea water from a bucket tied to a rope, which she tossed and pulled up with the skill of an old pro.

Of course, she'd be naked. Indeed, she often liked to go around naked.

Her demeanor was so odd and nonchalant, so natural that you had to concentrate and look closely to tell whether she was naked or wearing her thigh-length blouse.

Her movements seemed to go beyond the barrier of clothing, so that there was little difference between when she was dressed or not, apart from the fact that her outline was clearer when nude.

The boy knew quite a bit about sailboats, and he could be trusted. He showed experience and skill – unlike a lot of young people who attend sailing courses and accumulate various certificates and licenses. When out on the seas, a lot of them lack the least bit of common sense, which is learned through practice and humility, and can be mastered only by actually sailing.

He wondered where the two of them had sailed. On what kind of boats had they gotten their experience?

Their folks had probably taken them to sea when they were very young.

But they didn't talk about the past.

It was as if they'd just hatched out of that inflatable – gorgeous, friendly, educated, polite and sailing experts – custom-designed company for Alex, trained to guide him back to reality.

He looked at the sails, then all around the horizon, 360 degrees. He saw the boy preparing a fishing line to toss in the water. At the same time he kept an eye on the sails, the direction of the wind, and the functioning of the automatic pilot.

His attention once again turned to Sophie. She had finished with her bath and was now combing her hair. He found her very attractive.

More than her beauty, which was not dazzling, it was the way she moved that enthralled, her unusual way of snuggling up close to him and transmitting her warmth and serenity. He did not need to squeeze her tightly, for she already knew how to become one with him.

After sailing alone for so long, he now had a trusted crew.

Alex got up and announced, "I'm going to sleep in the cabin, to get out of the sun. Last night I didn't sleep very well. After being at sea for so long, I'm not used to being in such busy waters – it agitates me, especially at night."

Then he added, turning to Adam, "Be careful, the southernmost Caribbean islands aren't far off. You know, where there are more boats than birds. If the wind picks up, you'll have to adjust the sails and even change course somewhat, if that helps you sail better. Then we can re-set everything once we decide where we really want to go. But we'll take care of that tomorrow."

"Don't worry. It's a pleasure to be sailing on such a well-balanced and generous boat. Good night," came the boy's ready response.

As he headed toward his cabin, he smiled at Sophie. She smiled back with a knowing intensity that filled her every move and expression.

How nice it was to be lying in his own bed, listening to the splashing of the water against the side of the hull, and at the same time feeling reassured by the fact that there was someone else manning the helm. He no longer had to leave the risk of colliding into something up to chance, and he didn't have to get up out of bed to make adjustments due to changes in the wind.

His arms and legs felt relaxed, and he wondered whether this really might have been the true end of his solitary searching.

He was drawing closer to home, by now approaching waters that were very familiar to him, amid islands flocked with tourists.

"For now I'll rest, and worry about the questions later." As such thoughts passed through his head, he turned on his side to fall asleep. But he heard footsteps inside the cabin, and the door slam shut.

He turned with a start.

Sophie was standing next to the bed, looking at him.

Without a word she was already astride him. She bent forward and covered his face with her hair. She took his face in her hands and began giving him tiny kisses on his nose, cheeks, forehead, neck. He felt himself drowning in her hair as it danced and caressed him, as Sophie wiggled about, kissing one cheek then the other, one side of his neck then the other, one ear then the other.

It all happened with such sweetness and delicacy.

She sat back up, relaxing on his belly.

Point blank she asked him, "Why are you sailing alone? What are you looking for? You're too intelligent a man to be sailing round the world simply for the sake of doing it."

He looked at her as if he had never seen her before. He felt as if he had been found out and stripped down to the bone.

He searched deep inside himself and wondered, "Should I tell her? I can't. She'll laugh. How would she ever understand? We've only just met." Though perhaps it wasn't true – they'd known each other for ages.

They had already lived some bizarre, distant experience together.

"I'll distract her, I'll kiss her, make love to her – there'll be time for explanations later."

Sure, it would all seem very natural – for the past few nights they had slept clinging to one another. She was sitting on top of him, naked and smiling with her face slightly bent to the left, waiting for an answer.

He raised his arms and placed his hands on her shoulders, as if to pull her toward him. As he did so, he heard himself saying in a very clear voice, "I'm sailing the seas to find out the color of the wind. And after two years, I'm more mixed up now than I was when I started."

Sophie broke from his grip and threw herself backward.

The tiny cabin filled with joyful laughter, long and sonorous.

Like a catapult, she once again bounced down upon him. She spread herself over him and began kissing him with a passion he would have never suspected from a being that emanated sensations of "warm serenity."

He felt he had been freed, in mind and body.

They were among the most intense minutes of his life. He seemed to feel tears running down his cheeks, but he couldn't tell whether they were his or hers.

Then, with the same smoothness with which she had lain upon him, Sophie sat up, on the edge of the bunk.

Looking at him with beaming eyes and barely able to conceal her enthusiasm, she said in a well enunciated fashion, as if affirming some important conception of life, "Adam and I left home for the same reason – we decided to travel the world in search of the color of the wind. And what's more – to see whether the wind has more than one color and language, beyond the way it appears and communicates with you."

She sat still, waiting to observe Alex's reaction.

He lay there, flabbergasted – especially considering the content of the second part of what she'd just said – "More than one color and language."

It was true.

Maybe this was the reason why he felt it was possible to communicate with clouds, storms, the sea, but never with the wind.

The wind came from afar, it carried its color and language quickly, and went by before one could learn to communicate with it.

"Well, what do you think?" she asked anxiously.

"I'm surprised. I think I've been wasting my time concentrating on just the color of the wind without first understanding its different languages. I feel illiterate."

She laughed – laughed with joy.

"Don't sweat it – in this world we're all more or less illiterate. Hold on, let me see if I can transmit to you some of my own heart's sensations about the wind, and you try to transmit yours to me. We can leave the language of the wind for tomorrow. The wind is a true polyglot."

She lay down beside him in that narrow space. They began kissing, touching one another, meshing with one another in the name of the color of the wind.

They may have been the first couple in the world to make love in order to exchange their sensations on the color of the wind.

Come to think of it – the world is old and varied. It hides things so that each time humanity rediscovers something, great joy is experienced. In all probability, they had not been the first.

Anyway, it was nice to think that they were living an almost unique experience, enjoying the most normal thing in the world – love.

As they made love, she spoke to him about the color of the wind.

"Close your eyes and open them on the inside. Look up toward the sky, let your mind follow them beyond yourself and beyond this cabin. Imagine the white sails against the blue of the sky – even if yours are stained with gray and a bit tattered. Now think of me, my kisses, the warmth of my body; of how close you feel right now to my inner self, because you're physically inside of me.

"Don't move and think of the wind. You can feel the blood running through your body and at this moment thicken in your genitals. You imagine the same thing happening with me.

"Blood is red. Isn't it as though you could see it? And that its red color is a much more intense, ruby red in the part of your body where it pulsates the most? Can't you see it, above and all around your sails, a pinkish light from the east, which continues westward? Toward the east the color is more intense, then it fades as it goes along, until it meets up with your sails, where it becomes redder, more vivid. Behind the sails remains a pale red color, which blends in with the sky.

"After, it becomes light pink and whips toward the west.

"Your sails have robbed a bit of the wind's strength, they've become swollen and throbbing, just like you.

"Wait.

"Talk to the wind, through the flowing of your blood and the view of your internal eyes, which gaze up at the sky in search of changes in color.

"Squeeze me tight, listen to my pulsating, kiss me and imagine that the more excitement you give me, the faster my blood flows.

"Move slowly and imagine my blood becoming redder and more intense. The intensity of the wind increases as its color becomes more and more intense."

He seemed in ecstasy, yet tense and incredulous that all this was happening to him, out there in the middle of the ocean, after his attempt at fleeing from everyone and everything.

The boat leaned further to one side and began to produce the classic sounds one hears when the wind picks up and puts everything under tension. She placed two fingers upon his eyes.

"Don't open them. Adam will take care of it. You keep looking at the sky from inside yourself, going beyond this cabin."

He heard a loud noise.

Adam loosened the sails and adjusted the boat's course.

The lapping of the waves against the hull had become more insistent.

The boat shook as it raced along, taking its pleasure as the tension became stronger.

He saw the sky grow redder and redder, almost ruby red. Dark red, very intense in the hollow of the sails, an orangish blend behind the boat, and red, red and more red as it faded into the sky.

The wind blew strong and steady.

Alex was surrounded by red.

His hands dug into the warm, smooth skin.

She took her hand from his eyes and squeezed him with both her arms.

He whispered, "Thank you for showing me the color of the wind."

He opened his eyes and kissed her.

The color of the wind disappeared, taking the most intense part of love-making with it.

He lay still, having for the moment decided not to provide any explanations as to why the wind invoked by Sophie had remained so strong and rife with tension; why inside of him the sensation persisted that Sophie's presence had accelerated the flow of his blood and had kept it flowing so quickly with her gaze; why the wind was red, like blood.

He opened the door of the cabin, crossed the front room and looked out.

The wind was blowing stiff, Adam gave him the okay sign with one hand, and flashed him a smile of satisfaction.

"Go back and take it easy, everything's under control here. We're moving pretty fast." Strange, the wind had suddenly picked up without any visible change in the sky. It was a good wind – a trade wind from afar.

"I cut back a little on the jib. Tonight we'll have to choose our destination."

"Call me if you need any help. And whatever you do, don't leave the cockpit."

Adam nodded.

Alex returned to the cabin, closed the door and lay back down next to Sophie. She looked upon him with a somewhat challenging glare, which was, however, softened by her peaceful eyes – an expression that seemed to say, "See that – you wanted wind and now you've got it. You wanted to talk to the wind, and I've given you the chance. You wanted to see the color of the wind – and now you've seen it!"

All he said was, "Tomorrow we'll talk about what's going on inside your head. Right now I've got to collect my wits from today's experience and try to understand what I've seen and felt; try to figure out what really happened."

"I'm in no hurry. Sleep easy. I'm no witch, and even if I were, I'd be a good witch. I'd never harm anyone as sweet as you."

"Are you sure about that?"

"As sure as sure can be," replied Sophie.

He kissed her on the shoulder.

Chapter 14

The next morning they did not decide what route to take. They continued in the direction which made best use of the wind. They reefed the mainsail to straighten the boat and not expose it to excessive strain.

He loved his boat, his true companion for a long time now.

Whichever way they went, it was still more or less in the right direction: northerly. They did not bother to study the maps and plot out a precise course.

They just took a quick look to check the route they were on. They could take it easy, for there was still only water ahead of the bow.

Land and its dangers, the islands, lay not along their route. If they continued this way, they would leave them leeward. It was a thrill to think they were living to the rhythm of the wind, and if they kept going would eventually reach the top of the world.

Each of them, in his or her own way, tried to latch onto a dialogue with the wind.

They spied on the wind to see if they could discover its color.

Alex was excited, yet he really did not understand why.

His interest in figuring out the language of the wind, however, soon began to dwindle. As for the color – he had seen it quite clearly the night before when Sophie snuggled up beside him and pointed out the different patches of sky sectioned off by the sails, speaking to him with great intensity – Alex could see those shades of red. He felt as if he were actually immersed in the wind.

Oddly enough, this also happened when he was inside his cabin and he could perceive the wind only through the force it exerted on the sails, on the structure of the boat, and by the beating of the waves against the hull.

He closed his eyes, held her tight, breathed in an atmosphere tinged with many shades of red. He felt his blood pulsating and had the distinct sensation he could feel hers as well.

Then he went on deck, observed the horizon, touched the taut sheets, talked to Adam, who was bursting with enthusiasm over how well the sails were trimmed.

Adam was even more electrified than Alex, and said, "This wind is really something! It's been steady for nearly three days. Strange sky. It seems to have its own plan of action which has nothing at all in common with this wind. I've never seen a phenomenon like this before. It's as if the wind were just around *us*, and those clouds to the west didn't even realize it. They look placid, fluffy. The sea has gotten a little rougher, but not in proportion to this wind. It's a wind that comes from nearby, though to the east you have to cross a helluva lot of ocean before you reach Africa. I don't think I've seen any storms on the horizon, but then again storms wouldn't blow so steadily for so long. There must surely be a front not far from us, but for the past three days it doesn't seem like the sky has changed, and there haven't been any signs of any front. The barometer is high and holding steady. You want to turn on the radio?"

"Absolutely not, I'm enjoying this sailing as if it were my last, as if we were headed toward a hole in the ocean that's going to swallow us up. I'm sorry, I shouldn't be talking like that to you. You're young, you're burning with desire to live life."

Adam stared into his eyes for a few seconds then calmly replied to Alex's last observation.

"I'm young and happy. I love everything, I'm psyched about everything. Sometimes I think I'm like this because I take part in the things of this world only partially, almost like an observer. I remember what fascinates me and try to forget the rest. A lot of the time it gets me down, because I know that the further on I go in life, the less chance I'll have of keeping this game of mine up. Maybe a giant hole in the ocean would be an intense experience, of nearly biblical dimensions, which would pose an exciting and definitive solution to my worries about the future."

He laughed heartily, with shimmering eyes, as if he could see this immense blue vortex beyond the bow, with the red wind whipping all around it.

He took off his cap, ran a hand through his thick black hair, and whispered, "Why not?"

Alex had the sensation that the boy's personality was much stronger than his own.

He felt like he was in the presence of a cheerful and pure force that was trying to teach him something.

His spirit shook for a second.

Those two excited him, they attracted him, though they could also make him feel a little self-conscious.

Perhaps it was their disarming simplicity. How many times had Alex found himself in the world somewhere looking for simplicity in all things and in his relationships with others?

Very often it seemed as if he had succeeded, but then he fell right back into the system, making colorless and all too complicated compromises.

Was the wind red like the blood of life, or colorless, as it filled the voids left by compromises among the elements of nature and its creatures?

"You're right. Why not?"

He got himself a glass of water and relaxed in the cockpit. He felt exhausted, without knowing why. It had been a long time since he had spent such a pleasant stint, and with such little work to do.

Sophie and Adam took care of practically everything themselves, while all Alex did was play the role of captain.

They were in open sea, sailing with a steady wind, along an easy route, in a well-tested boat – what was there for the captain to do?

* * *

In life, an exciting situation that becomes drawn out for a lengthy period of time – no matter how pleasant it may be – puts a person's constancy to the test.

Odd, how people can be. When peace reigns, they want to argue. When war ravages, they want peace. If the calm and excitement alternate, people become unaware of time passing, and as they age, they mutter away – but it is acceptable.

Good, strong wind, sails taut as in a dream, the sea steady, the course steady: Too much of everything to be real.

Perhaps at this point they could have accepted the challenge of the vortex in the ocean – or more simply, they would have appreciated a change in the weather, a different shade of red.

That night as he lay clinging to Sophie, Alex began complaining about how the wind was carrying them north too fast, drawing him toward home – and he wasn't yet ready to deal with problems of returning.

He was very irritable.

He seemed to be back in the days when he would go sailing to relax between one business deal and the next.

He wondered aloud, "Where are we going and why are we in such a hurry? I have to plot a course. What shall we do?"

"Alex, didn't you tell me you'd gone to sea with the intention of not plotting any course? Maybe we've woken you from your dream, caused problems for you?"

"No... I think you've just re-awakened some old sensations."

"Ah, I see what you mean. Have you lost interest in the color of the wind, now that you've found it out?"

"I don't know whether I've seen the true color of the wind or whether it was only what you think the color of the wind is. Maybe each one of us sees it differently. Maybe the wind is colorless because it must adapt to the natural world that surrounds it, because it must help the elements blend and live together. It could be the wind that goes around exciting and calming people and nature. That way, time passes almost unobserved, in an alternation of small compromises in order to steer clear of tensions and clashes that are too big and destructive. Only sometimes it can't diversify as it would like to, so it gets mad and the situation gets out of hand – then come the catastrophes."

"What are you saying? I can hardly follow you. Take it easy. And as you calm down, so will the wind. I promise. We'll spend tomorrow on the deck talking about these theories of yours on the world, and when you think you'll be heading home, and toward what island you want to head. We'll just chill out and talk very calmly, as the wind becomes a simple breeze which will fill the sails but also give us time to decide."

They made love, but it wasn't like the first time, at least for Alex. He started off enraged, but her sweetness pervaded him. He became shy, then felt himself sink into her world full of "warmth and serenity."

He fell into a deep sleep. When he awoke all was still dark. The wind had calmed down.

He got up to adjust the sails and the automatic pilot with Adam. He turned the bow westerly, in the direction of the islands.

He thought, "Who knows how long it's been since the wind calmed down? That's funny, I usually perceive even the smallest changes from inside the cabin, even when I'm sleeping. Could the wind have stopped all of a sudden, just like that?"

He turned to Adam and said, "I have the impression that the chances of our meeting up with the giant vortex, the hole in the sea, have pretty much vanished. I don't get it though – the sky looks more or less the same, as far as I can see. Do you know whether the wind died down all of a sudden or not?"

"I don't know, I must have dozed off. Ask Sophie. Tomorrow we can tie ourselves to the boat and go for a swim. I can't wait. I'm glad we're in for a nice calm day – and that we'll be able to savor even more being all alone out here in the middle of the ocean."

"Go ahead, you get some sleep. I'll stay out here for a couple hours."

"Thanks."

Adam went below – which was something he rarely did.

He stretched out on the couch and went to sleep.

Sophie shouted so Alex would hear her, "Aren't you coming back to bed?"

"No, I just relieved Adam – told him to go to his bunk. I don't know why, actually. It's just a typical sailor thing to do."

Two minutes later Sophie stepped out through the companion way and sat down beside him.

She wore a simple white cotton blouse and had brought her pillow and blanket with her.

"Look at the sky. No moon. The stars are shining so bright, they seem so near. Tell me their names if you know them."

Alex recalled the Florida skies, where the stars looked like screws with lit up heads, screwed into the vault of the heavens to hold it up.

Out on the open sea they were even brighter.

"Sophie, I'd rather just look and not talk. And feel you near me, take in the sea, enjoy this much longed for solitude and let myself be transported by time, in silence until tomorrow morning."

"You're right," she said, snuggling up to Alex's body the way only she knew how.

They spent the night united, living happily ever after... until morning.

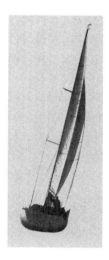

Chapter 15

The morning sun found them half asleep on the deck. The boat moved along slowly, the sails undecided whether to fill with the light breeze or go limp.

The sky was magnificent.

The calm sea inspired good cheer, as did the sensation that the breeze was strengthening and growing more determined, promising a pleasant temperature even at midday.

Their course would become smoother and would put an end to the sails' indecision.

They looked around, then took turns wetting their hands and faces in a bucket of seawater. After freshening up, they drank a hot cup of tea. The liquid gas for the stove did not betray them, though they were down to their last drops.

Alex and Sophie then sat together in the cockpit, fully aware that they had to talk and make a few decisions.

The most important of these – where to go? Their supplies were practically down to nothing. The islands were not far off.

Which island to head for?

There were independent islands, French islands, American islands, tiny islands, crowded islands, jet-set islands, and big islands that didn't seem like islands at all.

Neither of them seemed to want to seriously discuss the matter.

Instead they sought to convince one another of who had had the best times and travels on those seas that they knew so well.

At one point Sophie said something as if she had just recalled it at that instant, "We have an appointment with a boat that's docked in Antigua this month, in Port Nelson."

Alex suddenly felt ill at ease.

He had no real reason to, but felt that an obscure shadow was just then passing over his spirit.

These two beings had so unexpectedly appeared in his life, and he got on so well with them. He hadn't yet posed the problem – where were they going, what kind of plans did they have?

It seemed as though this were only the beginning. What were a few days compared to that long period of solitude that he'd spent at sea?

And now she enounced that phrase with great precision, "We have an appointment in Antigua."

That black cloud – was it jealousy?

Who was he jealous of? Did he think these two beings belonged to him? As long as he had lived, he'd never imagined being able to control someone else.

It was something he couldn't conceive of.

It must have just been a bit of regret, because he understood that this beautiful interlude in his journey was about to come to an end.

"I'd give the world to find out what you are thinking right now." As she pronounced these words, Sophie watched Alex intensely, with a curious smile.

"I'll tell you later. Give me a minute to find our location with the GPS, that way I can adjust the course and sails, and let you know whether you'll be able to hop that boat by the end of the month. Right now I don't even know what day it is. Come on, let me be a civilized ship's captain."

Then he got up and went to work, helped by Adam.

The boat took a new course, more westerly. They were sailing with the wind almost from the stern; going was slower now. Alex returned to the cockpit.

"It's going to get hot. Anyway, I've found out it's 10:20 a.m. U.S. Eastern Standard Time, November 14. Depending on the wind, we should reach the strait between Guadeloupe and Antigua in about three and a half or four days. You'll get there in time for your appointment. There are even three hours of fuel left for the engine, in case we have to speed up our entry into the harbor, or if the wind dies down when we're in sight of the islands."

"You've become Mr. Efficient all of a sudden. A minute ago you didn't even know where you were. I haven't seen you use the GPS once this whole time. Now you're acting like the pilot on a commercial flight. I guess you really want to get rid of us."

"What are you talking about? It's the exact opposite. But a certain feeling has taken hold of me. Sailing, sailing and sailing just doesn't interest me anymore. Right now I feel like I've been wasting too much time in solitude, being hungry and thirsty and wet. I have no further intentions of suffering seasickness and sometimes even the fear of…who knows what – maybe the fear of being so small and at the mercy of the waves, tossing me about as if I were nothing. They kicked me, they slapped me around – and unperturbed I smiled and said to myself over and over again, 'How I love being out to sea.'

"It's true that once the storm or the dead calm has passed, and the intense rain or tropical heat has gone, and the wind begins to blow just right, and the sea sparkles as if with a light all its own – you forget about the sad times and you get right back into it. You're free and happy again. Really – when people ask whether I've been caught in dangerous storms, I usually say I don't recall even one, and it's true. But since I've been out to sea for quite a while, of course I've run into a few bad storms. I remember the beautiful moments, like a climber who's reached the top of the mountain and forgets how hard the climb was. But inside me there remains the vague awareness of all the hardships and suffering I endured.

"Enough! I want to go back to living with people. I don't care anymore about the color of the wind and its language.

Within the mechanism of the world that surrounds us, this is just another deception like all the rest."

He spoke with conviction, taking himself by surprise. But perhaps it wasn't a decision. He couldn't have decided anything. He couldn't deny all his sacrifices, and those imposed upon those around him.

It was an outlet.

He was headed toward a port. There was a deadline to be met. There were two human beings on board with him.

He had to admit it – the new situation was enticing.

He had regained his daring and decision of old, from before he had cut himself off.

When it came down to it, his life had always been an ongoing search, filled with experiences whose results were either positive or negative, but always real and illuminating.

His journey was nearing its end, not only geographically but also intellectually.

Luckily, the two spheres happened to coincide.

Absorbed in his thoughts, he looked out upon the sea, not knowing where else to rest his gaze. Sophie ran a hand through his hair, nudging him to turn his head toward her. With a calm but firm voice, staring him down penetratingly, she said to him simply, "I'm glad you understand."

It was late afternoon on November 17, with the sun on its way to its nightly repose. They were sailing north of the flat, low Gran-Terre, and turned toward the high and rocky cape of the Basse-Terre. What a contradiction in names!

They dropped anchor at Gran Anse, along the magical northeastern coast of Guadeloupe – an island that to this day is enwrapped in a veil of mystery, nourished by its beliefs, kept safe by its high mountains, forests, springs and nearly black coasts. That bay gave them the opportunity to live one more intense night, as if they were alone in the world, and to take in Guadeloupe's overbearing personality.

A few other boats crossed their path, but these did not interrupt their thoughts. They'd drop anchor at sunset and would set sail at dawn, without a trace. The dark mass of the island would protect them from the rest of the world the whole night through.

The next day at Port Nelson in Antigua they would have to deal with all kinds of marine traffic and customs details, though there might also be the luxury of being served a meal in a restaurant awaiting them. They would purchase supplies and talk to the people.

Alex would introduce himself to the crew of the boat that Sophie and Adam were to board. Then he'd be left alone, but in a different state of mind. He'd then head even faster toward Florida, just as he once used to do, on his way back to work. This time, however, he had no appointments to keep.

And yet, he felt he had to hurry, caught up by a sudden fury that grew inside of him, that made him consider this stop at Guadeloupe on par with a Sunday outing – to be enjoyed to the fullest, because soon it would be over.

Good humor was a must, and enjoying the time that remained for all that it was worth.

But it's hard to have a thoroughly good time when all you want to do is…have a thoroughly good time, whatever the cost. Like New Year's Eve – you have to party it up.

But it's different when the happiness and satisfaction of such and such a moment arises suddenly, from who knows where.

Indeed, that night was tinged with melancholy.
Of course, embraces and heartfelt words oozed forth.
There's the re-emergence of the key to the world system, the human being – "heartfelt words."
He thought of the words of a hero of his youth, the great Italian poet Giacomo Leopardi:

His mother and father
Console him for being born.
Then as he grows,
They both support him,
Go on trying, with actions and words,
To give him heart,
Console him merely for being human...

* * *

Although tired and with her sails clearly showing the fatigue she had been exposed to, the boat made her way into the old English port of Antigua showing off all her grit and beauty.

They doubled round the cape of that well-protected harbor. Upon seeing the old British fortifications, Alex was caught up in a whirlwind of emotion, as he thought of the golden age of sailing and the feats of such a strong-willed seaman as Lord Nelson.

He had already been moved coming round the cape, only this time it was much more intense. As far as the hardships of sea life were concerned, he had lived through them all. He felt great respect for those who had blocked the port of Brest, as they crisscrossed for months along the coast in cold, stormy waters. All they could do was gaze upon the French coast and desire food and beautiful women. All they had to do was guess that the English coast, their home, was very near.

They sailed and sailed on, over and over again passed along the same stretch of sea, as it rained, beneath the sun, through the wind, storms and dead calm. It seemed as if he had lived with them. What it came down to was a temporal mix-up, not an experience. He was now in a harbor where many of these sailors had surely been anchored for days, on the same vessels used to hold back the exuberance of Napoleon.

As they headed toward their anchoring place, they decided to furl the jib, turn on the engine and drop the mainsail. The propeller was covered with marine vegetation; it was tough going for the boat.

But once inside the inlet, the scene changed.

Toward the end of the main docks they could make out the old British barracks, while everywhere were sailboats of all kinds and colors.

Here was the tourist's Caribbean, in all its great ferment.

They looked one another in the eye without a word, then looked once again upon the boats, the dinghies, that went back and forth to shore, the people.

They looked for a place to drop anchor.

All together they burst out laughing – not knowing whether out of joy, relief, disappointment or sadness.

To be sure, laughter often hides sadness. They laughed without conviction, without blaming or appreciating.

Adam moved toward the bow to maneuver the anchor.

After a few minutes Alex yelled, "Drop anchor!"

As if an accomplice, he said to Sophie, "We're early. You must be happy. You've got all the time you want to greet your friends… and say goodbye to me."

She kissed him and whispered, "Do you believe in good-byes? Or better yet, do you think you can control the whole mechanism of good-byes, adieus, farewells, re-encounters? I like you because you're always so direct and explicit. You're great! Tonight I aim to send you off with all the attention a ship's captain deserves."

"You even tease me now that you're back to where you wanted."

She made no reply.

She ducked into the cabin with her simple, beautiful figure, her warm skin, her loose movements.

He entered to find her straightening her things out. She had fixed her hair and looked dazzling.

She was dressed.

Chapter 16

Chatting and laughing they walked, commenting, observing, almost as if they had arrived from another planet and wanted to immerse themselves in Antigua's tourist life.

There were little shops, restaurants, people dressed in a whole array of colors. Then there were the smells – smells so different from those carried along by the sea wind.

Alex felt that there was something intrinsically false about this new experience of theirs.

He had the clear sensation that Sophie and Adam moved about as if they were at home, among faces very familiar to them.

He had been to Antigua many times and sooner or later was bound to run into someone he knew among all the crews strolling about the port.

Theirs, however, was a different kind of relationship with the surroundings. His would have been chance meetings, while Sophie and Adam, though they kept up their tourist attitude, gave the impression of being in a place that was extremely familiar to them.

He also noted the difference in the attitude of the Antiguans toward them, with respect to the way mere tourists were dealt with.

They decided to look for a good restaurant. They were longing for a complete meal; they desired to be waited on and drink some good wine. Thus, they had inflated Alex's dinghy, which he kept in bags in the bow. It even had an outboard motor. About halfway there, they ran out of gas and had to row. The day was nearly over by the time they climbed ashore. But they were in excellent spirits, because they knew they would find fuel in the port and motor back to Alex's boat sated and satisfied.

Inside the restaurant, the food and wine dissipated reflection and doubts.

They truly enjoyed themselves.

They talked at great length, about nothing and everything. They laughed, enjoyed a good many toasts, squeezed one another's hands many times, if only just to touch each other.

Alex wanted to pay, and though he had cash with him, he decided he'd see whether his credit cards still worked. When the waiter returned with the receipt requiring only his signature, it was his confirmation of having returned to life the way it used to be.

It was the final test.

But had he returned to the system or had he been sucked back into it? These were two different ways of interpreting the same reality.

Their table was off in a corner, semi-hidden from the rest of the dining room. They got up and headed toward the door, their faces glowing with satisfaction.

Alex recalled Sophie's promise regarding that night, and wondered whether she had remembered.

Sophie drew near the door, followed by Adam.

Alex returned to the table for his pouch-bag and his sunglasses, which he'd left amid the empty glasses.

He turned and saw a very New England couple in their forties get up from their table and kiss Sophie and Adam.

He watched them from afar. He wanted to better understand the other half of the world that these ex-searchers for the color of the wind belonged to.

It was instinctive to think of all of them, including himself, as ex-something. It was by now clear to him that that obsession was linked to a past experience, to which his new friends also belonged.

After all, whether it was their aim or not, they had been the ones to make him realize that his feelings regarding the solitary life he'd led on his boat had evolved.

The four of them spoke quite leisurely, though they talked of something important to be sure, as could be easily seen by the attentive way they looked at one another and participated in the conversation. Sophie nodded at least twice, making to the two people before her a gift of her smiles – smiles that conjured up images of a warm sunrise over a turquoise sea. As they went on speaking, that attention, which could also have concealed strong apprehension, turned to satisfaction.

Sophie turned to look at Alex. He understood that the time had come to gather his things together and head toward the door.

The four of them shook hands quickly, almost nonchalantly.

They were fully at ease now, as if they had gotten what they were looking for. When Alex got back to the table, the couple had just sat down. They nodded to him, maintaining an apparently cordial smile. He smiled back, fell in behind Adam, and the three of them left.

"Do they belong to the group of friends your appointment on the boat is with?" Alex asked with a certain disinterest. In reality, though, he was very curious.

"Yes and no. They may come with us. Or they may stay here."

"Do they live here? They seemed very interested in you, I mean, almost worried about something."

"We've known each other for years; we see each other often."

Sophie took him by the hand and set off running toward the inflatable. "Come, my captain – that's enough chatter."

As soon as he had dropped them off at the boat, Adam asked if he could take the inflatable back to shore.

He would return the following morning – not too early, he specified – to pick up the documents filled out by the authorities, and help find a slip on the dock and necessary supplies.

"What service," said Alex. "Thanks."

He added nothing more, nor asked questions on how the boy intended to do all this.

Adam just smiled with a certain satisfaction. As Alex had figured, in that port, he was quite at home.

The next day they would probably be lined up on the dock, alongside many other boats. Who could tell how his companion of thousands of miles of water would react? The queen of splendid anchorages in solitary bays would now be steeped in among her own kind. Alex would even see if he could find a diver to clean its propeller and bottom.

He felt so close to his true companion, the boat, that for a while he actually forgot about Sophie.

She understood. She left him alone outside to take in all those objects that are so strange for one who does not live on the sea, but are so alive and meaningful for a seaman.

She heard him talking. But he was not talking to himself or to her. He was communicating with his true travel companion.

About a half hour later he made his way down to the cabin. The boat had now surrounded him completely; it enveloped him. He felt safe.

He whispered to Sophie, "I hope I can make you feel the way she makes me feel." He hugged Sophie's warm body tightly. Now she seemed tinier and more supple than ever.

Part Three

Chapter 17

He was once again alone at sea. Little wind, a nice day. He passed between St. John and St. Thomas. With the latter astern, he proceeded west-northwest.

He had sailed along the island coasts, from Antigua to St. John. Twice he dropped anchor in bays full of boats. Each time, he pulled in during the afternoon and left the next morning.

No one had ever bothered about him.

He was all too happy to be sailing along the coasts of various islands, and remembered the vacations he'd spent there sailing with his wife and kids, when they were still little.

There had been a young sailor by the name of Roberto, a sensitive soul with a passion for the sea running through his veins. He would transmit a very simple message – we're all on this boat, and we must do everything we can to make this trip safe and enjoyable.

Roberto had just turned 18 when Alex met him. Then he got married and began a brilliant career. But he had remained very close to Alex and his family. Even today, Alex's eyes moistened when he recalled those trips.

How his children loved riding on the inflatable and meeting the people aboard the other boats.

Sometimes Alex left them anchored in a bay with Roberto while he went to work for 10 days. He couldn't wait to join them once again.

In those days the family was united not only by love, but also by the games they played and fun they had.

Now, each member was into his or her own thing. He felt as if he had been abandoned.

He had always been the driving force behind the family's desire to do new things.

Then he became merely their fulcrum for serious business – work, organizational problems, the personal relationships and tensions that cropped up as a result, the celebration of events and holidays, suggestions and advice…

The love that had bound them remained. Love, though, went hand in hand with being committed to helping them all on their way.

What had happened to those days when they used to play together? When they would wander around on the inflatable in search of new adventures, when they would go fishing and explore the bottom of the sea wearing diving masks.

Nothing in particular ever happened, but it all seemed like such a wonderful adventure, at the end of which they would all re-unite round the dinner table, ravaged with hunger and content to devour whatever had been whipped up on the spur of the moment.

These were the things he was thinking as he saw the islands float by. As a result, he felt the determination to revive what was boiling up inside him and start over.

He put together a plan: When he got back to Florida, he wanted to spend more time with his kids and laugh wholeheartedly – at least during the weekends.

In any case, he had returned to sailing as in the days of old – GPS always turned on, always knowing where he was and trying to reach whatever place he sought out by the shortest, fastest route. What's more, he had enough fuel to get him near the coast of Florida, if there wasn't enough wind. He made use of the generator.

He turned on the lights, cooked, kept the fridge on. There was water, wine, pasta, bread, eggs and oil aplenty.

He still hadn't had the courage to use the phone. He knew it worked, though – the dial tone was loud and clear. Talking. Asking and answering questions. Explaining. Hearing news – no, he wasn't ready for all that.

Perhaps he was waiting for some kind of sign, a push, anything that forced him to react.

It happened the day after he left the Virgin Islands. In order to get home "faster" (a word that belonged to his old life), he'd decided to go from St. Thomas toward the Old Bahamas Channel, passing north of Hispaniola, then cut along the South Bahamas Bank and into the Florida Strait.

He'd pull into Key West, where he'd go through customs, which for U.S. boats was not very complicated.

He'd stop for a couple days to get a whiff of the Gulf of Mexico, and then, one day later, would arrive home.

At last, he had a plan!

He had been sucked back into the system – and, strangely enough, he was happy for it!

But why, then, had he been wandering around all this time? He smiled and thought, "Easy! So that I could learn that on this planet, there's no life without a plan."

The wind all but ceased. The ocean was like glass, the sails fluttered.

He rolled in the jib, sheeted in tightly the mainsail, turned the engine on low, so that it wouldn't make too much noise. The boat began to move slowly.

He felt the urge to take a nap.

Sea, all around. The automatic pilot kept the boat on course with ease.

He lay down in the cockpit and fell into a deep sleep.

He was so relaxed that he forgot all that had been on his mind. He could no longer hear the hum of the engine or the rhythmic flapping of the mainsail, and not even the roar of the large outboard motor of the inflatable that had begun circling his.

Nor was he awakened by the cries of the people aboard that boat.

Usually he heard everything, even the slightest sound, the slightest change in the wind or waves.

Perhaps he felt he was already at home. His mind raced.

He had no idea how long he had slept, but at a certain point he awoke with someone banging on the side of his boat, as if there were someone knocking on his door, followed by the distinct sound of human voices.

At first he tried to think who it could be. Then he realized he was still on his boat. This relieved him.

Had he dropped anchor, or was he in open sea?

Who was knocking?

He heard the sound of a large outboard motor buzzing near him on low. There was also the hum of another craft.

He grew worried. Instinctively he raised his head from the cockpit, and found himself before two faces that emerged from alongside his boat. One was a man's face, the other was a woman's. Both wore helmets with microphones attached. With their left hands they held onto the toe rail, while their right hands bore firearms steadily.

All three looked at one another.

Alex didn't know whether he should be scared or not. He noticed they were more tense than he was.

One of the two then announced, in an authoritarian tone with a marked southern accent, "United States Coast Guard, sir! Do not touch any weapons you may have."

Alex smiled. His face was content and relaxed.

The officer added, "May we come aboard?"

"Of course you can, with pleasure. I was sleeping. You caught me by surprise! Gee, you look like Martians! Tie up to the stern."

"No need to. Just three of us will climb aboard, the rest of the crew will stay on the inflatable and follow us."

As they cautiously made their way on board, Alex noticed a large U.S. Coast Guard cutter a quarter of a mile off, with its red stripes, following ever so deliberately behind his boat.

Alex rose slowly.

He detested weapons and had no intention of giving those soldiers the smallest excuse to get angry.

As he wore only shorts and a T-shirt, it was obvious he was unarmed.

"Are there any weapons on board?"

"Yes. There's a rifle somewhere in the front cabin. I hope it hasn't completely rusted! Do you want to see it?"

"No, it doesn't matter. Is there anyone inside the cabins?"

"No, I'm by myself."

"May we take a look around? You stay here with me."

He ordered the others to check below and make sure Alex really was alone.

A few minutes later the man returned, saying everything was okay.

There was something strange in their manner. They were still suspicious, and listened carefully to what was coming in through the speakers inside their helmets, most likely from someone on the cutter that was following them.

The woman, who appeared to be second in command, pulled a document from her pocket – a computer print-out, with a couple photos.

She looked at the piece of paper, then eyed Alex carefully. She handed the paper to her companion in such a way as to prevent Alex from spying its contents. Then she asked, "What's your name? Can we see some I.D.?"

"Alex Mancini. I'm a U.S. citizen, and a Florida resident. If you let me go down inside, I'll get you my passport. I've been out to sea for the past two years, and now I'm on my way home. I guess I was sleeping pretty heavily – first time since I've been out here all by myself. It's just that everything's so calm, and home's getting near…"

"That's all right, Mr. Mancini. We're very glad to have found you and that you're going back home."

They relaxed, showed Alex the paper with his picture on it, and the boat's as well, and began to converse cheerfully with the cutter over the microphones incorporated in their helmets.

It was hot. Alex almost felt sorry for them, in their uniforms and heavy shoes.

The crew in the inflatable waved as they pulled in closer.

"Can you tell me the meaning of all this?"

"Does your radio work?"

"Yes."

"Turn it on, I'll give you the channel. Our skipper wants to talk to you himself."

Alex grew even more baffled. Then he thought of the worst – perhaps they were looking for him because they had bad news they needed to communicate. But they were all smiling! Maybe they didn't know anything, they'd just received the order to find him and were satisfied that their mission had been accomplished. The skipper surely knew more.

And there he was, on the radio.

After exchanging the first few formalities, the two decided to speak on a first-name basis – they were, after all, both sailors a long way from home.

The cutter had been at sea for three months, out of New York. It was working between the Caribbean and the Bahamas to ferret out smugglers headed for the United States.

When the skipper recognized Alex's boat, he tried calling on the radio several times. But since there was no answer, he sent a crew over to check out the situation. They were worried because it looked as though there were no one aboard. They feared something had happened to the crew, or that the boat had been stolen and there were persons on board who did not want to be seen. That's why they had moved with such caution until they recognized him – which they were able to do despite all the weight he'd lost.

They complimented one another on their respective vessels, and the long journeys they had undertaken. Then John, the cutter's commander, got to the point.

"I'm so glad we've found you."

"Why were you looking for me? Is there some kind of problem?"

"No problem, apart from you. Where the heck have you been this whole time? Your family's looking for you, they think you're lost – except for your wife, who swears you're an exceptional sailor and is absolutely convinced that you'll be back some day. And now I have the proof she's right."

Alex was very satisfied with this proof of Margareth's faith in him. And though they didn't always get along, they counted on one another. He felt a bit guilty for having left her alone for so long.

John continued, "You should also know that your paintings have made the big time, and that your idea about going off to try and find the color of the wind really captured the curiosity of the press. You've become famous, only no one knows where you are. This only increased the curiosity of the media. We knew you'd crossed the Panama Canal, and we'd had reports from other places, but you would always disappear in such a hurry that you'd become the obsession of the newspapers. That's why we're so glad we've found you! Are you really going back home?"

"Of course!"

"Judging from your speed, I wouldn't say you were in any big hurry! I was told you have a telephone – a high-power job. Why don't you use it? Afraid to reveal your position?"

"No, it's not that. I just have to concentrate to find the right words."

"Have you at least found out the color of the wind?" the skipper asked with a touch of irony.

"It's a complex thing, it can't be defined. There are so many variations and interpretations. I think for us seafarers it's a series of red shades, from pale to ruby red. When we close our eyes and force ourselves to imagine it, it's like being covered in purple and you're floating on the water. It's like blood, pulsating and flowing away. It sustains you to the last, then goes... and you, in the dead calm, see it flee away! You think, when you die you'll be with, it dressed in purple, as happy as can be.

"When I get back I'm going to write a little book. I'll send it to you as soon as it gets published – you're the first person from the 'real world' to ask me about my experience."

John did not exactly understand what Alex meant by the expression "real world." He did know, though, that Alex was a good sailor, a good designer and even a painter – even if he was a little weird. That explanation had left him speechless. At any rate, it wasn't up to him to judge.

He went on, "I have to get in touch with headquarters and report that I've found you. And that you're okay and headed toward Florida. What's your ETA?"

"I'll hit Key West in about a week. Three more days, I'll be home. Tell them I'll call in a couple days, and that I have discovered the color of the wind," he replied, laughing. "You know if my family's okay?" he added.

"Yes, as far as I know. The newspapers are usually loaded with stuff on other people's problems. Oh well, have a good trip! I'm glad to have spoken with you. I'll be waiting for the book. I'll send you my home address."

Alex thanked him profusely. He stood waving for a long while at both the crew in the inflatable, which was returning to the cutter, and the cutter itself, as it passed alongside him.

The cutter's crew waved back, some were whistling, yelling "Bravo!" Alex noted how the commander had taken his hat in his hand and was waving it with great professional dignity.

Once again he was alone.

He picked up speed and decided to fix something to eat. He might as well take advantage of calm seas, when it would be easier to cook himself up a tasty dish of pasta.

Chapter 18

He noted the metallic tune typical of electronic devices, as if it were coming from another dimension. It created a sense of alarm in him – he hadn't heard that sound in quite a while. Once he got over his befuddlement, he threw himself into searching for the telephone he'd left on since he'd run into that Coast Guard cutter two days earlier.

His hand hesitated to pick it up, but his blood ran quickly and his heart was as if turned to stone.

What was he going to say?

He knew who it was.

He had to gather his wits or, better yet, remember everything he'd already decided to say.

But there wasn't any time left.

He couldn't remember anything.

He pressed the button and said, "Hello!"

"I heard you're on your way back – I'm so glad! Why didn't you call me? I found out from the Coast Guard and the newspapers. At first I was very happy, but then a little offended, since you hadn't told me yourself. I thought, maybe your phone was broken. But I said, why not try to call? – and here you are on the other end!"

Margareth's voice came through loud and clear.

She continued, "At least you're alive! It's getting harder and harder to understand you! I had to use all my inner strength to come up with some explanations and go on living like a normal woman."

"Were you able to?"

"Is that all you have to say after all this time? You were out to sea, combating the elements, coping with problems and overcoming obstacles that you yourself created. I didn't know whether I was Mrs. Mancini or Widow Mancini, whether I could fall in love with someone else or had to wait for you... and the children..."

Alex heard in her words the entire history of their relationship, and decided to take the offensive.

His fugitive life, just him and his boat, was over.

All of a sudden he clearly realized that he was now back to where he'd started. He had come full circle.

The clasp in the chain of his travels was about to close.

"Margareth, please, let me explain. When I left I told you that you were free to do whatever you wanted. I signed a bunch of papers, took care of all the financial issues, gave my consent to a divorce if you wanted one. This whole thing has to be a lot simpler, or perhaps awfully complex. As far as you and I are concerned, we've just got a few questions to answer. Are you glad I'm back? Do you want me back home? Do you still care about me? What do you want to do? I've already asked myself these questions. The reason I never called you was that I didn't know how to go about bringing up the subject, I didn't want to influence you one way or the other."

"Can you tell me how you thought you were going to influence me after being away for so long?"

"Simple," replied Alex calmly, "if I had called you all happy and mushy-mushy, telling you I was on my way home, you would have felt embarrassed to express what you really thought. If you shared in my state of mind, our conversation would have been a thrilling exchange of loving words, indulgent questions, enthusiasm and warm feelings. But if your life had changed in the meantime, think of the difficulty I would have put you in. It's better that you get it out of your system immediately. Now I know you're the same old Margareth. You haven't decided anything, you're awaiting my return to throw my defects in my face and point out my virtues, so that it's me that pushes you to make a decision. Welcome back, Margareth!"

Several moments of silence followed.

Perhaps she had taken offense, perhaps she was mulling things over.

Strange, she always had a ready come-back and she never let you finish what you were saying.

Something was eating at her. She had to think before deciding what to say.

The pause was only a short one, however. She began more energetically than before to sustain her theories. She eventually wound up crying and saying she loved him. She had missed him, yet his distance also had a soothing effect on her.

Yes, he had truly found the old Margareth.

A few hours later he received a call from Pamela. She was almost formal, but very curious about his experience at sea. A friend had told her about it.

Only toward the end did she say in her truly sexy voice, "I'm dying to see you. Come visit as soon as you can!"

Who knows whether the invitation had come out of mere curiosity, or the true desire to see him?

Alex remained quite cold and decided he'd clear up this doubt once he'd gotten back.

He spoke with his children. He asked them a heap of questions. He also told them exactly when he'd be arriving, and his plans on what he was going to do once he'd gotten home.

He called his closest collaborators at work and a few friends.

After many years of working together and knowing one another, each conversation was extremely pleasant. He found out everything he wanted. He gave them simple but precise answers.

He was satisfied.

He couldn't wait to see all of them again!

He reached Key West in good time. Mentally, he was a bit weary. Meanwhile, the telephone kept on ringing.

He wasn't used to talking for so long anymore, and listening to so many human voices and the thoughts of so many different people.

He was used to talking to the sea, the sky, the clouds, and perhaps even to the wind.

There had been dolphins and birds, but they communicated only to tell of the life they led. They had no desire to influence you, much less annoy you.

He heard him say to himself, "Welcome home, Alex!" He thought this might be a fitting title to a book, if he ever wrote one, or a painting. Only, what to paint?

He was certain, though, that once he found himself before a canvas the subject would become all too clear to him.

In any case, he was ready to get back into worldly affairs and everyday life. He was enticed by the possibilities. But now his awareness had grown, he would live differently.

He smiled.

Though how sure was he that he would now live so differently?

* * *

He spent the last day of his adventure sailing off the coast of Florida, in his Gulf of Mexico of old.

A fair wind was blowing from the east. Land was not far off, the sea was calm. Sunset reminded him of his walks on the beach – nighttime, nearly a full moon, thinking things over in his anchored boat.

The next morning he drew so near the coastline that he could see the windblown treetops.

The waters were very shallow, but he felt at home. He knew how to navigate in those waters.

He looked at the houses. Though the land was low, it cut off a good bit of wind. On the other hand, the sea was nice and calm, like a lagoon. He could hear the water caressing the bow.

The wind was little more than a cross-breeze. Going was smooth and efficient. The gulf had welcomed him with open arms.

Crouched down on some cushions, before his eyes passed – as if in a documentary film – beaches, stretches of trees, isolated houses, small cities with tall buildings, access channels to lagoons, and more trees and isolated houses.

The whole scene was very familiar to him, and he was enjoying it down to the smallest detail.

After arriving in Key West he kept in continuous telephone contact with his children and the office. They knew exactly where he was and had reserved a spot for him to land in one of the city's busiest marinas.

He figured he'd be entering the lagoon around noon.

He'd drop anchor in a bay near the entrance canal, get himself and the boat together, and at 5 p.m. would enter the marina.

Chapter 19

Just a few meters left to the dock. What a great crowd of people had gathered! There were even vans from the major TV stations with antennas on their roofs.

An almost festive air abounded. It was all so unreal – comical actually.

"Good God! Pulling in by myself to the dock, amid all those poles and confusion! This boat was made to sail the seas, not to zigzag among these traps."

He drew closer and recognized Margareth, several friends and people from the office. As the bow touched the dock he saw his two sons hop aboard with lines. He shifted into reverse. His kids yelled, "Hi, Dad! We'll take care of everything, turn off the engine!"

They busied themselves with the boat, pulled other lines. As he made his way among the crowd, virtually incredulous, among all these faces he knew so well, he realized his beloved boat was now up against the dock, tied up and going nowhere.

Margareth climbed aboard. They kissed. Applause rang out.

He began shaking hands, and as soon as he could, squeezed the arm or shoulder of his boys, as if to reassure himself that they were there in the flesh and doing fine.

Two years and one month had passed. He walked off the boat and onto the dock. He felt as if he had arrived from Mars. The faces of the others were just as he'd remembered. Nothing at all, actually, seemed to have changed. He was the only one who was different. He understood this by the way they greeted him and looked at him. He had lost a lot of weight.

During his trip he had bought T-shirts and pants here and there, and had cut and taken in those he'd had already. At Key West he'd gone to a barber shop. He bought some new things, trendy even. Nevertheless, it was not enough to turn him back into the Alex he was before setting out.

His expression, his gaze, too, were different. For everyone else, two years had passed. For him, a lifetime.

What was it that made this event so intense that you could read it on people's faces? It seemed as if they were looking for something, and that they were looking for it in him, Alex, and in that boat of his, which had been put to the test.

Of course, two years alone on the high seas was not such a big deal. Many others had sailed round the world, across difficult routes, setting new world records.

No one really knew which route he had taken, and few had asked themselves whether he had gone round Cape Horn or crossed the Strait of Magellan to get from the Pacific to the Atlantic. It didn't matter. His had been an adventure of the spirit, not a regatta. As far as they were concerned, Alex could have tooled around the Gulf of Mexico for two years and it would have been the same thing.

What was it, then, that fascinated these people so?

Sailors usually tried to reach some destination, or had some precise goal in mind – like setting a new record, putting oneself to the test, assessing one's own resistance, or simply visiting new places and having fun.

It's a weekend kind of thing – you hop in the car or on your boat, and take off already knowing where you're headed.

Alex had escaped from that world.

The only aim he'd had was to remain at sea to get away from all his daily, routine influences, and subject himself only to the impositions of nature.

He was no hero, he hadn't sought to challenge nature. On the contrary, he had tried to give himself up to it, surviving day by day, any way he could. He had nothing to prove, no goals to reach, no records to break.

Survival was enough for him, being alone, thinking, and perhaps even learning the color of the wind.

And yet, nobody could believe he'd set out to discover what color the wind is. They were all convinced that he was concealing the actual, deeper motivation behind his voyage.

And they had come to make sure of that, in person.

Each of us has at least one unanswered question tucked away in his or her heart.

Was it better not to think about it, just work and live, or should one take time out to reflect and risk being overwhelmed by anxiety?

Perhaps these people would find inspiration in Alex's face, in his eyes, in his words.

The press had built up people's curiosity by talking about the weirdness of such a feat. Scholars were interviewed and debated the peculiarity of the mission – finding out the color of the wind.

Many people took that mission to heart, they had identified with Alex – they could put themselves in his place. And though they remained at home, they had sailed with him and experienced the very same doubts.

All this appeared quite clear by the expressions on their faces, their questions, their comments, and by the attention with which they observed him that day on the dock.

But the people who knew him, or those who thought they knew him because they had had contact with him and had followed along on his adventure, wanted to find out what had changed in him.

What was that mad search for the color of the wind really a cover for?

Was it what they too were looking for? The same desire, only lived more intensely?

It must have been something extremely unique and important if it was worth subjecting oneself to so many hardships and sacrifices.

Not everyone was able to get a clear focus on the problem. They were curious to learn something they still did not have a firm grasp on.

Before them stood a man who had searched and searched – but for what?

Had he found anything?

And had he returned to prove something?

Perhaps he, with his obsessive desire to discover the color of the wind, had at least succeeded in comprehending the sense of these questions.

Everybody, when it came down to it, realized that this was the most they could ever aspire to.

The answers would always remain a secret hidden within each of their hearts.

* * *

A marvelous reception had been set up in the banquet hall of the marina. Lots of talking, hugging, interviews, a little kidding around, a bit of teary-eyed emotion.

Alex felt immediately at ease. He had been re-inserted into his old world without any trouble at all. He longed to go home, but knew that for the moment he had to take part in this event in order to satisfy people's curiosity. Everything was working exactly as it had before his departure!

He had been born and raised in that system; he knew the script by heart.

Some people spoke on a microphone, greeting him in various ways. They made friendly allusions to the content of his journey and showed curiosity especially with regard to the main issue at hand – what color is the wind?

By the way they spoke, it was clear no one expected a real answer just yet, but only a few words on the subject.

The microphone was handed to him.

What struck him most was the silence that fell upon the hall. The whole place seemed to have frozen in an instant.

He felt gripped by fear. What did they expect him to say that was so important?

Doubtless he would disappoint them.

He gathered his strength and figured it was best to lighten the atmosphere with a joke. Instead, he heard an unsteady voice coming out of his mouth, which said, "I discovered so much beauty, but it was also extremely exhausting. I lived a lot of life out there. Though it got pretty lonely sometimes." He stopped, sought to keep things a bit more upbeat, but a journalist in the front row asked him, "Would you do it over again?"

"No."

"Why not?"

"I'm through with seasickness, and land-sickness too. Anyhow, throughout my life I've always tried to overcome my experiences mentally. I have a need to move on. My one regret is that I'll never again receive as warm a reception as this. I can't tell you what joy you've given me. Words cannot express my gratitude. I can feel your friendship, I'm happy.

But I can't figure out why you've gone to such great lengths here. What have I done that's so important? All I did was wander around for a while on the sea, which I love so much. It's not that big a deal."

The laughter among the crowd broke the tension a bit. Then came the much awaited question, "May I ask you if you've succeeded in finding out the color of the wind? There's been a lot written about it, could you please give us a clue?"

Alex embraced the hall with his gaze. He felt as if he were being indicted, as if everyone there were thinking the same thought, "We demand an answer! You can't go off hog wild like that, shoving the whole thing in our faces, without owning up!"

"Such blunt questions, hard to answer. It's as if you were asking me to solve every doubt in my life, and perhaps yours as well, in a couple minutes, during a celebration among friends."

There was a murmuring of approval. He had hit the nail on the head when it came to the reason why everyone had come out that day, to celebrate a true sailing event, within the sun-filled and colorful setting of the marina.

Many among the crowd realized that this was neither the time nor the place for such a specific question, which surely demanded a fairly drawn out explanation in response.

Alex guided things back to where he could feel a little more comfortable.

"At any rate," he said, "I plan to write a book detailing my experiences, in the hope that somebody will get something out of it. For now, I can tell you this: There's not just one color of the wind. And its language may be interpreted in many ways. It reaches us from afar, brushes up against you and moves on. It's a kind of force that seeks to harmonize nature's elements – first by exciting them, mixing them up. Then, as before, it leaves them to battle it out among themselves.

It's hard to have a relationship with the wind. It's much easier to talk to the sea, the clouds, and even easier to talk to pelicans, seagulls, dolphins and all the rest.

The color of the wind is its secret. You might guess it, but it's hard to see. It flees because it comes from so far away. It enwraps you, then it's off, leaving you alone. When you begin to focus in on it, it's already gone.

I highly recommend these sensations – you've got to experience them. All you have to do is go a few miles off the coast and imagine you're just a link in the chain of life on this planet. You'll begin talking with the sea, and the sea will answer back! Then, very slowly, you'll concentrate on the sky, the clouds. They'll understand you, too. The wind will brush up against you. But do not suppose that you'll be able to easily communicate with it, or learn its mysteries.

This is an extremely healthy exercise.

The wind caresses and shakes you, makes you feel like a link in the chain of nature, then it goes away and leaves you alone – thus forcing you to get in touch with the relationship that connects you to the other links.

The only thing that matters is that your mind, your spirit – call it what you will – can manage to follow all this movement and ask itself why, as if it were something outside yourself. Its role is like the prompter feeding the actors their lines on stage – involved in the entire process without the obligation of having to face directly the ruthless judgment of the audience. Even if the prompter does his job well, things can still go awry. And even if we think good thoughts, the harmony of nature may break before our very eyes and blow us into extinction. But deep inside, we still think we're waiting for another act to begin, whether our eyes are open or closed.

"That's right, open or closed, the wind envelops us, it makes itself felt and leaves. But we are sure it will return.

"We do not know whether it will reappear violently or softly. We'll just have to wait and see – see if we can somehow influence this rhythm by communicating with the wind and following the analysis of its colors.

"I guarantee that this can happen – but how to make it happen and for how long, is a mystery."

Total silence.

Some had understood everything. Others believed to have understood. And others, disconcerted, asked themselves what that man was saying, what language he was speaking. There followed a few moments of embarrassment, which finally muted into applause, at first timid, then decidedly enthusiastic.

Another journalist asked, "Why do you want to write a book on this experience? What does it have to do with the color of the wind? Why don't you paint it! Paint the color of the wind!"

Alex replied calmly, "I'll try." He then thanked everyone from the bottom of his heart and joined his friends to relish their presence. He now realized how much he'd missed them.

He spent that evening with his family, talking about lots of things, enjoying the company of those dearest to him and eating a good, hot meal with them.

That night, dazed and confused by this whole series of experiences, he found himself in his big bed, alongside his wife. The sheets were clean. And nothing moved, not even the light on the nightstand. For a second he had the sensation that he was a mummy being placed inside a sarcophagus for all eternity. Only, he did not know what eternity was yet. So he was still just Alex in a real bed.

The bed was the same as when he'd left. So was his wife. He had lost a lot of weight, though. His muscles were hard and taut.

It would take many caresses from Margareth and many nights among freshly washed bedding to see if he could abandon himself completely to the tranquility of sleep.

Chapter 20

Day after day he began rediscovering his life – a beautiful, spacious home filled with every comfort; the ever stimulating company of his wife; talking with friends; his close relationships with his sons; his exchanges with co-workers; the usual restaurants; concerts; comfortable trips, which led to new experiences and reminded him of past experiences.

Then, the pleasure of painting.

His paintings were now shown in many cities round the world, and this gave him great satisfaction.

He took frequent vacations with Margareth. They wandered about Europe, Asia and South America.

He also saw Pamela. Once he spent a week with her in Bermuda – a good midway point between the U.K. and the U.S. He hoped that being alone with her on an island in the middle of the ocean would give him a chance to see the red of the wind again, and to feel it pulsating through his veins. And more than that, he hoped Pamela would share in this experience with him.

It was a wonderful and involving stay together with a rich exchange of ideas and sensations.

But he never saw the color of the wind again.

When in Florida he worked, painted, and enjoyed chatting with his wife, who was as busy with her own life as always. Then there were his children and work – they'd learned to get on just fine without his continuous intervention.

One boy had married a brunette who was very much on her toes; the other seemed headed down the same track – with a slender blonde.

He was not a grandfather yet, and it didn't look like he would become one any time soon. This was one more reason to feel young. He felt like he still had his whole life ahead of him.

He often thought of death, though without dramatizing it. Actually, he was curious about it.

By now, many of his relatives and friends had passed away. Often, he would imagine the parties he'd be attending with them once he'd closed his eyes for good...

But then he would focus back on his daily routine, on work. He liked to indulge himself by thinking of things that would happen – even when he could not be certain that they would. Think up something and it will probably happen – the problem is when and where. The wait only distances you; it may take more than one lifetime. You drag yourself from mood to mood without seeing any conclusion. Then, it may happen that all or part of what you imagined unexpectedly comes true. But a moment later it's already forgotten, and you get the feeling that what just occurred, occurred because of destiny. There's nothing you can do about it. The gratification that comes with having succeeded dies down and eventually becomes one more brick in the building of your existence.

In the end, you wonder whether this was truly as important as other experiences.

Alex often asked himself, "Why did I undergo all those sacrifices for two years? Was it worth sleeping badly, going hungry, wasting so much energy? Was it worth all the hot and cold, the dampness? Having to cope with moments of great discomfort when you're in the middle of storms and raging elements? When you're putting your own faculties to the test amid a sea of solitude?"

He had seen how one basic theory of life had been proven through him – that everything winds down and reaches a dead point, stalls out. Then everything starts back up again, driven by the force of man's will and courage. It's a natural cycle, perhaps it occurs throughout the universe.

Suddenly he interrupted his reflections.

He wished to know exactly what "universe" really meant. Indeed, he thought about this fairly frequently and realized he had no idea at all what the word meant and was not even able to imagine it.

At least he was aware of this limitation – which is crucial to our development. We consume ourselves, aware that we're going on and on, until we realize that our mechanism has worn down. We discover this along the way; all it takes is a little reflection. Who knows whether the natural elements realize that they, too, follow the very same path as we do?

The current of el Niño, the snow that covers mountaintops – are they aware of how temporary their existences are?

He had traveled much, done much, reflected much, and wasted so much energy, only to find himself once again with his bike on the same beach, looking for the thoughts he'd left buried in the sand.

Where to start over? Was he perhaps to discover that perpetual motion is just an illusion on this earth?

The sea, the waves – they seemed so different to him. He'd seen too much. Best to just go back home and relax in a lounge chair amid an oasis of greenery, maybe even watch television.

Alex had great respect for television – it was the strongest and safest sleeping pill he knew.

All it needed was a timer to shut it off automatically after one hour.

He wrote a book on the color of the wind, which was published by a big publishing house. They believed that Alex's experience would spark readers' interest. But the book was less successful than had been hoped for. The color of the wind and the theme of traveling for traveling's sake were no longer in fashion.

People's curiosity had faded as soon as his adventure had come to an end. Reporters found new stories to slake the thirst of the public and their editors.

Three years had passed since his return. Those closest to him began to notice changes in his behavior. In two months' time his attitude had become a genuine source of concern. Alex responded evasively to their questions, acted strangely.

He had become somewhat lazy and vague – he who had always been so careful and tireless in making new plans and taking them to their conclusion. The people around him began to think he was plotting a hare-brained adventure similar to the one he'd pulled three years earlier. Only, they couldn't figure out why he seemed to have all but given up sailing, though he did speak often of the sea. He'd put his boat in dry dock. Now and then he'd go to see her, to touch her.

He talked to her. He climbed up the ladder, checked on her. He paid a person to keep her in perfect working order, and ordered that she should be ready to set sail at any moment, except for the final coat of antifouling on the bottom hull. His family and friends said, "Maybe he's planning another voyage."

One evening he invited his wife and two sons, along with his closest collaborators and friends, to a fine dinner, held inside one of the private dining rooms at a local restaurant. At mid-meal he stood up with his glass in hand and proposed a toast, announcing tersely, "I must set out on yet another experience. I'm leaving in a month."

The only ones who'd known about this beforehand were his lawyer and his accountant, who were dear friends. With them he had gone over all the legal and financial questions, which were dealt with based on the experience afforded by his last great adventure. He wanted to be sure that his absence would create no problems as far as jealousy and power struggles were concerned.

He gave his two consultants and friends a nod, then continued his speech, "That's right, in one month. This time I'll be traveling like a regular tourist – going by plane, car, ship, boat, even on horseback if need be. Which is to say, I plan on traveling in the most convenient and comfortable way possible. I'll sleep in hotels, apartments, bungalows, and so forth. I'll stay in touch with you, as if I were on a normal business trip, over satellite phones or regular phones, by email and fax.

During this trip I'll also be trying to meet new people for possible future collaborations. I'll keep you constantly updated and give you instructions as to the handling of any negotiations I've launched. We'll talk at least once a week."

One of his sons asked, "Do you have a specific destination in mind or are you just going to wing it?"

He hesitated for a moment before answering. He sat down, placed his glass on the table and replied, "I'll be making concentric circles, beginning at a point and progressively distancing myself from it as I go. If I'm not satisfied, I'll move the center and begin a new series of concentric circles. My aim is to scour the world.

"Who knows whether I'll stop once I've explored everything, or sooner? I do know that I'll understand when it's time to come home – or rather, my spirit will know.

"My absence may last a month, a year, five years, or even longer. But one day I'll come back. You'll always be able to count on me, and if my presence is required here, I'll temporarily interrupt my travels.

"It is my desire, however, that you're all free to think and act as you please, without worrying too much about me. Especially you, Margareth."

Margareth was taken aback for a moment, thinking how selfish Alex really was.

They looked one another in the eye for a long time. At last, their faces relaxed. For Margareth it was clear that between the two of them there was still something strong and deep. She also understood that, when it came down to it, with a husband like Alex, it was better to see a picture of him and talk to him on the phone rather than have him around all the time.

Alex was a difficult man, but he also had his good side. He would protect her always, and they knew they would be near one another at the hour of death. They thought of one another practically every day. But it was better to imagine Alex off somewhere, doing his own thing.

She asked him, "From your words we've learned that once again you're looking for something – would you mind telling us what?"

"I'm looking for… oh, it's tough to explain… I still don't have that many clear ideas. I'm looking for someone that has something to do with the wind."

All present looked as if an enormous question mark was painted on their faces. It was as if they wanted to say, "Why, it's become an obsession!"

Alex added, "Yes, it is an obsession for something that I have not fully understood. I still don't even know whether this person really exists – I'm looking for a warm woman named Sophie."

183

Afterword

I literally grew up in a motor vehicle factory.

Day after day, from my earliest childhood, I lived amid the production lines of all sorts of two-, three- and four-wheel vehicles. The factory churned out quantities of motorcycles, mini-vans, and later, the famous Isetta – an egg-shaped city vehicle with a front door that opened in such a way as to allow entry without ever having to bend down. We then moved to building sports cars (the various IsoRivolta models), snow mobiles, and a series of Formula 1 racers (the IsoRivolta Marlboro) – just to name a few of our sexiest products.

The factory, our home and the extensive tree-covered grounds were all surrounded by the same wall, and life there was a kind of symbiosis of these three elements. The entire complex occupied most of downtown Bresso, a small town outside Milan, Italy. Inside that little world, successes and problems united people, animals and things.

Two well-defined classes of people gravitated round the facilities. There were those who were part of the factory organization, who either spent their days at the plant or worked beyond the gates to defend the firm's colors in other parts of Italy and abroad; and there were those from the outside world who came to us – customers, visitors and journalists. The former felt as if they belonged to one big family – a feeling that most of them retained even after moving on (myself included). The "outsiders," who often hailed from far and wide, were always thought of as friends of the business and the family and were treated accordingly.

With them, they brought a variety of customs, as well as problems that needed solving, and most of all, a boundless store of enthusiasm which, indeed, proved contagious. You see, at our factory we produced some very special, unique objects that men often fell in love with – perhaps because they had wheels and could be driven; perhaps because they went fast and never talked back.

My father had a magnetic personality and was extremely generous. He died in 1966 at the age of 57, during a slump in the business. I was 25 at the time, a newlywed with a degree in mechanical engineering that I'd received less than a year before from the Polytechnic University of Milan. I had to shift into high gear while still mourning the loss of my dad, whose passing left a scar in me that has never completely vanished.

Luckily, during my university years I had only attended those afternoon application sessions in which attendance was mandatory, while my mornings were spent at the plant. Even as a youngster, my favorite after-school activity had always been hanging round the factory. I still have warm memories of the friendships I made there. Though I never got the highest grades, I breezed through my engineering studies thanks to the rich human and practical experience I had gained inside my father's factory. Upon his passing I took the helm and was caught up by the same frenzy that had marked his life. I burned with the desire to create, to take risks; I had inherited a credo of seeking out new experiences, knowledge, and sensations. Joy came in making new and beautiful things that procured happiness for us as well as for others. Most of all, my father had transmitted to me the longing to always be a free man, to be the master, as far as it is possible, of one's own destiny, able to assume life's responsibilities without being overly influenced by boards of directors, important committees, religions and, especially, political ideologies and politics in general. His lifestyle had shown me that one could ignore geographical and cultural boundaries artificially set up by men, and look at the world with a much broader perspective. This vision of life, which he handed down to me, has led me along paths that at times have been quite difficult, paths where one is sometimes left standing powerless and looking on as positive human power is squandered and lost.

After experiences in different parts of Italy and the world, I literally dropped anchor – I arrived via sailboat – in the beautiful and cultured city of Sarasota, which lies on Florida's west coast, looking out across the Gulf of Mexico. It is here I hope to remain, until one day my ashes are dispersed by the waters of the Gulf.

I still keep that memory of the big yellow villa, my home in the green, wooded estate outside Milan, and of my life in that busy industrial city of northern Italy. My family still owns an apartment on the ground floor of the old villa, with a bit of yard just for ourselves, amid what has become Renzo Rivolta Park. I return every so often, when I can manage a break from my hectic schedule, and the place is like a safe, quiet oasis for me, where I am soothed by the house's thick walls, the trees I know one by one because I have watched them grow; some I even planted myself.

The need for open space and freedom inculcated in me by my father, along with his own strange physical need for adrenaline, have driven me to seek out a life brimming with experiences and changes. To begin with, I brushed aside all the rules which people usually adhere to if they want to make a successful career for themselves or simply become rich. The first of these rules is build yourself a resume, a business card that clearly identifies who you are, what you do and how you do it. You work to make this resume more and more credible, until you reach a point where the system itself just drags you along. As long as you don't make any huge blunders, you've passed the test – you don't have to be first in the class any more, or prove that you yourself actually ever attain all that you set out to.

A publisher once asked me to write the story of my life. Who knows whether I'll ever have the time, or even whether it's been interesting enough to entertain readers? For now, I'd be stuck in finding a fil rouge to make the whole thing comprehensible. All I can put on my business card is my name and the name of the company I work for, which are one and the same. There is one single constant in my life, though: the straightforwardness and stubbornness with which I cope with life's daily challenges.

On the work front, I've built sports cars, snowmobiles and Formula 1 racers; I've raised horses in the country and managed a riding stable; I've designed and developed a variety of transport vehicles, including quadricycles, electric cars and buses. I've even organized music festivals, one of which I am particularly proud: La Musica, the International Chamber Music Festival in Sarasota. Over the years, I have constructed factories and directed a large textile mill; I have built office and apartment buildings, fairly large-sized communities, shopping centers, and marinas; I have co-founded a bank. For many years I served as president of a prestigious golf club with a 36-hole course, one of my firm's projects (despite the fact that I don't actually play golf – I had to put up quite a front before various committees and at governors' meetings!). My latest madness involved the design and construction of yachts.

I'm no longer a young fellow, but I still have plenty of projects in the hopper.

All this surely runs against the grain when it comes to the cultural and economic trends of our times. Today success is measured more in terms of quantity than quality. And it seems that only a precise, repetitive and unrelenting marketing image can succeed in reaching sought-after sales results. This way of thinking doesn't bother me in the slightest, it's just that, unfortunately, I can't apply it – I can't live it. I consider this one of my limitations.

Sometimes I ask myself how I've been able to survive, keep my own company going (which, even though it is small, continues to enjoy excellent health) and to progress. I think that while quantity may mean business, passion and quality are protected by the spirit that makes the world go round. I look out and gaze upon the city lights in the distance and listen to the far-off hum, entranced, indulging myself in the awareness of being a poet, in the same sense that we can all be poets.

I felt these reflections on my own life were important because *Alex and the Color of the Wind* is but a simple story written by a man who sees, thinks and acts with great simplicity and believes that such simplicity is part of the world's true poetry. I don't mean only written poetry, but those magical moments in which thought, nature, rationality, efficiency, human relationships, battles, tragedies, victories, conquests, gains, losses, illnesses, quarrels, and good times remind us that it's all just a game we can always get out of – not always unscathed, but in any case, we do get out. We just have to open our eyes and try to understand that behind any complicated situation lies a simple explanation. Perhaps too simple to be grasped, since for centuries we've been taught to reason according to very complex schemes. It is only by complicating simple things that people with no particular talent succeed in controlling the world. Let's take a minute out and think it over. We may get lucky. Lightning may strike and ignite, within our minds, a flash of poetry, of creation.

In 1999 Crocetti Editore, of Milan, published a book of my poetry and prose entitled *Just One Scent, the Rest is God*, which was distributed in Italy and the U.S. One reader told me that it made him feel good to go back and reread a few passages during a special time in his life. I hope that you, too, will be able to say the same of this book.

Piero Rivolta
Winter 2007

Acknowledgments

It is very important for me to acknowledge all the people who have been so patient to put up with me in the process of transforming a manuscript into a real book. Unfortunately, the only way I know how to interpret my thoughts is to put them down on paper with fountain pen; I am very meticulous in what I write, but my handwriting is horrible. I hope Bill Gates will forgive me.

A special thank-you goes to John Rugman, an American who has chosen to live in Turin, Italy, for his translation of my book into English. Cristina Visconti has been an invaluable aid to me in more than just the publication of this book. Vanessa Houston has been patient and judicious in her support. Chris Angermann has helped with editing and shepherding this book to the printer. And last, but not least, thanks to my dear long-time friend Richard Storm, who continues to take care of my public relationship, even though he is semi-retired. He has contributed his sage advice at various milestones along this journey.